A Message For

All Time

A Novel by Donald C. Hancock

This story began
with a short story
and became a long
story. May your
story be as happy
as this one!
Don Hancock
Jan. 2015

DEDICATION

I lovingly dedicate this book to my wife, Finetta, who has always been the wind beneath my wings. She proof read the manuscript and helped in many other ways. I also acknowledge the help and encouragement that I received from my fellow writers on a writers' site called Helium. Lastly, I also thank the following friends who read my story and made helpful comments - Dorothy Ashe, Tom Carpenter, Chris Lupica, Marcia Scaggs, Heidi Piester, Kat Apf, Glory Lennon, and Patty Padgett.

INTRODUCTION

It is with great pleasure that I introduce you to Richard and Gloria. They are the primary characters of a little short story that just seemed too expansive to remain a short story. There was too much to see and do and the short story just would not stand still for it.

I enjoy writing on an authors' site called Helium. The story about the "message for all time" was first posted there, and it just seemed to shout to become more than a short story. It is a story of the patriotism that springs from living through a world war. It is a story of compassion felt for those who suffered loss during that war. There is a relationship between a single mother and her son that is inspiring to observe. And there is a romance between two people who had given up hope of having marital bliss after the death of their former spouse.

So, here is what it has become in its full growth. I hope that you will be as captured by the beginning chapter as I was. I gratefully acknowledge the help of my wife, Finetta, in proof reading each page and in encouraging me during the writing process.

I have enjoyed the writing of my first novel and I must say that the characters really did take on a life of their own and I awoke each morning with the ideas for the next chapter. I was not sure "what they were going to do" until they did it!

Donald Hancock. September 2010. Augusta, Georgia.

Chapter 1. "A Message Found".

Richard was celebrating his 17th birthday. It was Friday, July 16, 1954. He and his mother, Gloria, were staying for the week end at a cottage, owned by a friend, at Brighton Beach on the southern coast of England. On this marvelous afternoon He could hardly contain himself as he rowed his little boat to shore. He had found the proverbial "message in a bottle". He was afraid to try to open it in the boat for fear that he might damage the message. The bottle seemed obviously very old. The cork seal also seemed somewhat primitive by modern standards.

When he had secured his boat he put the bottle in his back pack, jumped on his bike, and headed for the cottage. As he ran into the house he yelled, "Mom! Mom! Wait 'til you see what I found!" Richard went to the kitchen table, the center of all things important in his family's tradition. He put down some newspapers and placed the bottle under the strong table light. He had difficulty with the cork at first but found a cork screw and got it free in a few minutes. He tried to "dump" the message but it, being rolled up, had unrolled and expanded. It would not come out without persuasion. He gingerly fished it out with some long eyebrow tweezers and carefully unrolled the brittle paper onto the table.

He read the following note to his mother. "I write these words to no one special. I have no family, except for one. But somehow it makes dying easier if you say some sort of last words. I don't expect anybody to find this so I write it as a statement to the 'cloud of witnesses' that the Bible says is watching me. I am floating in a little rubber life raft. The supplies aboard have long ago been used up, except for this bit of paper and pencil and a bottle that I saved. My ship went down from a German sub. Most of my buddies went down with the ship."

" Three of us found this dinghy. The other two, Bob Swithers and Melvin Dorster, have already died from exposure and, I think, loss of hope. We have counted twenty days. I am Jim Stark of London. I am very weak and feel that my time can be a matter of minutes or hours at the most."

" I want to say that I hope that what we are trying to do to turn Hitler around will work. I hope that peace will some day come back to the England that I love. But I want the world to know that, no matter who wins this war, I, Jim Stark, believe that freedom will win over tyranny wherever the two may meet. Freedom has within its own seed the fruit of triumph, and tyranny likewise has within its own seed the fruit of failure. God and the nature of life will see to that."

" And so I die with full confidence that my dying alone on this drifting sea is not in vain and I will watch the inevitable victory march of human freedom from some grand stand seat among my buddies, somewhere up there. Know that I die in full hope of living again. Love to all,

Jim Stark, March, 1942."

As Richard finished these words, he felt the tears welling up in his eyes. The tears surprised him at first and then he found himself thinking of several things about this experience that was affecting him in such a powerful way.

He realized that no one else in the whole world had seen these dying words of a man who thought he was speaking only to Heaven. Just he and his mother had been afforded the privilege. He was also reliving the poignancy of those war torn years and what they had meant to England and to the whole world. He was only four years old when this was written, but he had heard about these war years all of his life. And the pathos and suffering that was reflected in the note was, by itself, enough to bring tears to the eyes of anyone.

Richard's mother saw his tears and loved him even more for it. She knew his tender heart from his earliest days and always felt grateful that he had somehow inherited it from her own. They were both quiet for a long time, as though even a word spoken might dishonor the beauty of what they had just heard.

His mother finally broke the spell and said that she was wondering about how these men felt during those last days. Richard raised the question of the suffering that the loved ones had gone through during all of these years, not knowing anything about what had happened to these men.

Their families might not even know for certain that they are dead - only that they are "missing in action".

Richard went over the names again, Bob Swithers, Melvin Dorster, and Jim Stark. "You know, Mom, we know that Jim Stark lived right here in London. He said he just had one living relative, and of course, we don't know from what he said whether that was a mother or wife, or just what. But , you know what. I feel somehow that I owe it to Jim and to that one relative, whoever it was, to let them know what I found in this bottle today.

It's been twelve years but their loved ones could easily still be alive. Maybe it would help them to hear these words that we have just read. It is almost like, if I didn't try to find them and share this message with them, I would be letting those guys down."

Richard's mother said, "Son, I think you are right. In fact I feel very strongly that you need to find out if the other two men had relatives too. I am pretty sure they were from some where in England if not right here in London. I think we should write a letter to the Navy and see if we can find out anything at all about all three of them. Who knows what influence this message could have on the people who loved Bob and Melvin, and Jim.

Richard, I will help you in this if you want to tackle it. I can even take off from work if we need to do some traveling to follow up on what we find out from the Navy."

"Mom, Let's do it! I feel like we just have to do it. I don't think I could live with myself if I didn't at least try!"

Little did Richard and his mom realize how prophetic her statement would prove to be..."Who knows what influence this message could have on the people who loved Bob and Melvin and Jim."

Chapter 2. "After All These Years".

After lunch, that same Friday afternoon, they went to their home in London. They had just one thing in mind - calling the Royal Navy to see what she could find out about the writer of the message and his two friends. She looked for any information that she could find in the "Government section" of the London telephone book. There was a listing for the Royal Navy and she immediately dialed the number.

Gloria explained that she would like to speak with someone who could talk with her about persons who were missing in action during World War II. There was a long pause and then the operator said, "This is a most unusual request, Mum, but I will do my very best to find someone to help you. Please be patient with me, because the process might take some time. Could I call you back?" "Yes, of course" and Gloria gave her home telephone number. "OK, said the operator – please know that I will do my best but I might be calling a dozen people before I find the right person".

"I do appreciate anything you can do", replied Gloria. As Gloria waited, she rehearsed just what she would say. In about thirty minutes the phone rang and the operator said, "Mrs. Parsons?"

"Yes, this is Gloria Parsons."

"Mrs. Parsons, I believe I have someone who can help you. This is Sir Thomas Lawn, retired from the Royal Navy."
"Hello, Mrs. Parsons, How may I help you?"
Gloria thanked the gentleman and then told him the complete story from the very beginning.

Sir Thomas listened with intense interest and when she finished he cleared his throat and said, "What an absolutely marvelous story you have, Mrs. Parsons. Let me say that, ordinarily, the sort of information that you need can only be given to family members, but this is such an unusual set of circumstances that I promise I will help you if at all possible. So, we have three names – again, that is primarily Jim Stark, then Bob Swithers and Melvin Dorster, am I correct?"

"That is exactly correct, Sir!" Gloria was delighted that this person was obviously listening closely.

Sir Thomas continued. "Now, also, we do have some parameters concerning the sinking of the ship. The message was dated March, 1942, and Mr. Stark said that they had counted 20 days in their life boat. So that places the sinking either in February or March of 1942. We can search our records for any ships that were sunk within that time frame and search their lists of occupants."

"We can not be absolutely certain that the three were Navy personnel. According to my experience the ship could have been transporting combatants from another service branch.

But I will certainly begin with Naval records. Now, Mrs. Parsons, let me remind you that records were all kept in books in those days – no computers. Much of it was done in long hand. There were attempts to preserve all of the records after the war, but we certainly were not 100% successful. I promise you, though, that I will take this on as a high personal priority. I thank you very sincerely for bringing this to our attention."

"I can't tell you how much I appreciate your help, Sir Thomas!"

Gloria could hardly wait to tell Richard of her preliminary success! He was overjoyed!

He said, "Mom, in the mean time let's go through the phone book and see how many 'Starks', 'Swithers', and 'Dorsters' we can find. You never can tell. We might just luck up!"

They found only three 'Starks' and they were surprised at how few. There were five 'Swithers', and two 'Dorsters'. They realized, of course, that marriage might have changed the names of widows and daughters. By the end of the day they had called all of the prospective names and no one recognized any of the three men.

That night, at dinner, Gloria and Richard were both a bit discouraged. Richard said, "I guess we're being silly, Mom. This whole project could take weeks or even months. So there's no sense at all in getting upset because we struck out on the very first day!"

Gloria got up from her chair and came over to Richard's chair. "Son, before your Dad died, he said that you would be the 'man of the house'. Maybe you and I thought he was just trying to make you feel good. But, you know what? You have become a very mature young man. I really do admire and depend on your wisdom!"
"Thanks, Mom. You have no idea how good that..." Richard could not finish the sentence because of the flood of emotion. He stood up and they embraced for a long time, enjoying the strong bond that they felt.

As they stood, the phone rang. "Hello", Gloria speaks.

"Yes, Mrs. Parsons, This is Thomas Lawn. I do have some preliminary information for you and let me please emphasize that it is VERY preliminary. There is bad news and good news. The bad news is that there were just two ships sunk in the area during that time frame. One was a troop carrier, The HMS Doubleday, and we have a very complete record of its occupants. None of your three men were on that list. The other ship was a cruiser, the HMS Faraday. We have a partial list of its crew, but we do know that they picked up a partial replacement crew of ten men the week before and the list of those men was lost in the sinking. So your three could certainly have been among that replacement crew."

"The good news is that we have found the name of one 'James E. Stark' in the Naval records of that period, and his home address IS listed as London. Of course, after all these years this might be a very cold clue. But it IS a beginning!"

"The address we have is 25 Collingswood. The only name listed as dependent is a Mrs. Woolsey. It does not list what relationship she had to Stark. So that is it so far, Mrs. Parsons. I will keep at it. Please let me know if you have any luck with this address. I am as interested in the outcome as you are. This is a labor of love for me. I was a sailor too in those days!"

"Oh, thank you so much, Sir Thomas. I can not tell you how much this has helped! Even if this address does not lead us to our goal, it means so much to know you are helping us. We know that, as you said, it has been many years! Keep us informed and we will do the same with you!"

Chapter 3. "A First Success"

Gloria and Richard could hardly wait until the next day to begin their search for the address that Sir Thomas had given them. Then Richard remembered, "Blimey!" (Blimey was an old expression that his Dad often used and Richard loved to imitate. He and Gloria would always smile at each other when he said it)."Blimey! I just remembered that city map that I used for my school project. It has all of London with the streets listed!"

He went to the desk in the library and retrieved the map. Gloria brought a magnifying glass and he spread the map out on the kitchen table and turned on the over head light.

"Here is the list, let's see – The C's. Here it is - Collingswood! It's still there – C 4. I found it on the map, Mom! Do you have a pencil? OK – let's circle it so we can find it tomorrow without any trouble. Tomorrow is Saturday! You don't have to work! We can go after breakfast!"

Needless to say, neither Richard nor his mother slept very soundly and they both woke up before daylight. They had an early breakfast, got their baths, and then began the long wait before they could reasonably disturb the occupants of 25 Collingswood Place.

At 8:30 Gloria said, "I think we can go now. By the time we get there it will be 9:00. That should be fine."

They drove to the neighborhood with Richard looking at the map and telling Gloria where to turn. As they neared Collingswood Place, Richard said, "You know, all Sir Thomas said was 'Collingswood'. I do hope that Collingswood Place is it. It is definitely the only one by that name listed. So it is either the right one or else the right Collingswood is under some new freeway or parking lot!"

"No negative thinking on this project, Richard", said Gloria. "Here it is - # 25. It is an old house. This could really be it!" They went to the door and twisted an old fashioned spring type door bell. Gloria straightened her skirt and blouse. The door opened and an auburn haired woman who appeared to be in her 50's said, "Yes?"

Gloria took a deep breath. "I am Gloria Parsons and this is my son, Richard. We are looking for anyone who might have known a service man during the war by the name of Jim Stark..." Gloria was prepared to give a few more details, but the woman closed her eyes and looked as though she might collapse. Gloria and Richard quickly helped her to a chair on her porch. They each took an adjoining chair and waited until she composed herself. The woman finally spoke. "I knew Jim. What..What do you know about him? Is he alive?"

Gloria quietly said, "No. I am sorry to say, Jim died at sea as the result of his ship being sunk during the war." Gloria then told the story of the message being found and took out a copy of the message. She gave it to her son to read, knowing that a man's voice was more appropriate. She also felt that it was Richard's discovery and he deserved to be the reader. When he had finished there was that same silence that they had experienced when they had first heard the message. The message seemed to carry with it a need for a certain reverence.

After several moments, Gloria said, "when my son and I had finished reading the message, we felt strongly that we should try to find anyone whose heart ache might be relieved by hearing the story. Through the help of a Sir Thomas Lawn, we were able to obtain this address and also the name of a Mrs. Woolsey, who might have been related in some way to Mr. Stark."

The woman raised her hand, as though asking permission to speak. "Now it is my turn to tell you the part of the story that I know. I have not introduced myself, but I am Betsey Clark. You have absolutely no idea how much this message changes things! It is going to bring relief and sadness and a whole ocean of mixed emotions to the Mrs. Woolsey and to who knows how many others. But I hope that it will also open up Mrs. Woolsey's life that has been so closed for these twelve long years since she got the telegram telling of Jim's being missing."

"You see, Mrs. Woolsey, Clara, had been married to a sailor named Edward Woolsey. Edward and Jim had been close friends for many years, high school and after. Clara filled out the third part of 'the three musketeers'. Ed and Clara were high schools sweethearts."

"When the war started, Ed and Jim both decided to join the Navy together. Before they left, Ed and Clara decided to get married. Jim was 'Best Man' and I stood with Clara. I am Jim's first cousin, his only living relative."

"Ed and Clara only had a week together before he and Jim left for training. To everyone's sorrow, Ed was killed in a training accident during his first month in the Navy. Clara was totally devastated and Jim felt like he had lost a brother."

"Jim spent every leave he had with Clara. As I look back I really wonder if Jim had not been in love with Clara all along and just gave deference to Ed out of love for them both, because, within a six month period of time and before Jim shipped out the first time, a full blown romance had developed. They continued writing letters and during one of the times that Jim was back, he proposed to Clara and she accepted. They were planning to be married the next time that Jim came into port. But, sadly, there WAS no next time."

There was a long pause while all three – Gloria, Richard, and Betsey contemplated the double trauma that Clara had suffered in such a short time. Finally, Gloria asked, "Where is Clara now, Betsey?"

"Mentally, Clara is in a land of denial and hope. She has been unable to move forward with her life during these twelve years. She is still waiting for her Jim to come back and for their marriage to be consummated. I know that sounds almost crazy, but, you see, we know of several men who have come back after a ten year bout with amnesia. Clara just hopes that her Jim might just be one of these miracles. But, of course this changes everything. And who knows but that this might be the key that allows Clara to give herself permission to move on with her life!"

Chapter 4. "Pain From Having Loved".

Betsey has shared with Gloria that Clara has become frozen into a mental state of denial and hope – denial that her Jim could be dead and hope that he still might be one of the miracle ones who finally return. But this denial and hope has kept Clara's life from moving forward. She is still planning her wedding day!
"What is Clara doing?" asks Gloria. "Does she work?"

"Let me describe a day in the life of Clara Woolsey," suggests Betsey. "When she arises each morning she feeds her cat and then listens to the radio as she eats her breakfast – with one thing in mind – listening for any news that might have anything at all to do with Jim's where abouts. Then she scans the newspaper with the same purpose. After that Clara bathes, dresses, and goes downstairs to her cookie shop. Yes, she has an apartment over her shop."

"She has learned to function well enough in her job to satisfy her customers, but she goes through each day like a horse walking with blinders on. She has not had any semblance of a social life since the very day she received the news that Jim was missing."

"When she goes back upstairs she either sits, brooding over Jim, or else plans some intricate details of her wedding. Each day is the same as the last. She does that six days a week."

Gloria paused and then said, "Can you tell us where we can find Clara? Betsey, we promise that we will be as careful and considerate as we possibly can in presenting the news to her."

"I have no doubt about that," replies Betsey. "She lives in Guildford, 60 kilometers from here. You can get there in less than an hour."

"Yes, I have been to Guildford", said Gloria.

"Well her cookie shop is on Chapel Street. Anyone can tell you where that is. As I said, she lives in an apartment over the store. Generally, if she is not in one place she is in the other. She comes to London about once a month and always stays with me. I call her on the phone regularly to be sure she is OK."

Gloria stands and thanks Betsey. They all three have formed such a bond in their brief encounter that they all hug each other.

As they go out to the car, Gloria looks at her watch and she and Richard decide to have a brief lunch and then drive the 60 kilometers (roughly 30 miles) to Guildford. Betsey said that they could be there in less than an hour.

They decide to check by the shop and see what time she closes and then go back just before closing time to share their story.

They find the shop easily and look on the door to find the closing time. But they notice that there is no one in the shop but one gentleman behind the counter. So they go in and ask about Mrs. Woolsey. The clerk said that, ordinarily she would be there on Saturday afternoon, but that she was running low on some essential supplies and went to London before the providers closed for the week end. He was sorry to say that she would not be in the shop again until Monday morning.

Gloria and Richard went back to their car and laughed at the irony of their "two ships passing in the night!" Gloria said, "We need not worry my Dear! The longer I live, the more I am convinced that things like this happen for a reason." Richard said, "Me too, Mom. In fact, I just thought of something that I had not thought of before. When I was fishing the other day I was over by the jetty and had not caught anything at all. I had already decided to come in but then I looked over at one of the marker buoys and something told me to try over there. As soon as I reached that area I noticed the little bottle dancing in a puddle of foam."

"Oh, Richard, that gives me goosebumps all over. I am so glad you remembered that. So why don't we just go back to Betsey's. Maybe we are supposed to have Betsey's help in presenting this to Clara!"

They went back to London and pulled up in front of Betsey's house. They noticed another car out front. They went up on the porch , as they had before, and cranked the old door bell.

Betsey came to the door and, as she let them in, she whispered in their hearing, "Thank God!"

Betsey ushered her two new visitors towards a woman who was already seated and said, "Clara, I want you to meet Gloria and Richard. They went to Guildford this afternoon to see you and I assume they found Charley at your shop and he told them that you had come to London for the week end . They knew of our friendship and rightly assumed that you would be here."

"Now let me share with you all a confession. God has just answered one of those 'SOS' prayers that we sometimes flash at Him. Clara had just been here a few minutes and had already sensed that something was on my mind and was beginning to probe me for the cause. I was sitting here trying to decide the best way to begin and, I must admit, praying frantically, when you two rang the door bell. So now I can tell you, Clara, exactly what is 'on my mind'."

"This young man was out fishing just yesterday and he found a little bottle with a message in it. I am going to let him read the message and then they will tell you the rest of their story. I will tell you ahead of time that the message is going to make you very sad. But we are all here to help you get through it."

Clara sat rigid with her face showing a panorama of emotions, none of which included hope. There was dread, followed by fear, followed by panic and then resolution. With a trembling chin she quietly looked from Betsey to Gloria to Richard and said, "Well, I guess I'm ready." Then, as is typical of Clara, she smiled and said, "I hope!"

Chapter 5. "Telling Jim's Clara"

As these four new friends sat in the ambiance of this very old living room, their polite body language disguised the very active thought processes that were taking place. All thoughts were primarily about Clara.

Betsey's thoughts were, first of all, about the awful truth that was about to engulf her dear friend. She hoped with all her heart that this confrontation that she had been partly responsible for arranging would do more good than harm. At this point she certainly could not be certain of the outcome. She was deeply concerned for the safety of Clara's self hood. Yet, she was extremely relieved that she could share this responsibility with Gloria and Richard.

As Gloria looked at Clara she thought of the little smile that curled her lip and the gentle way that she had added "I hope" to her nervous statement that she was "ready". She felt that Clara was a young woman of great courage, who, in the face of information which promised to bring even more sadness into her already devastated life, was able to smile rather than give in to total panic.

She pictured Clara as she would have looked in a size 8 wedding dress if Jim had made it back that one last time. Now, she had probably added twenty pounds to that petite figure through testing her daily cookie recipes and the feeding of her sadness with comfort food. Her blond hair had been allowed to follow its own course with minimal care. She had apparently felt little need for make up. All in all, Clara was potentially a beautiful woman, both inside and out. But, certainly, inside and out were going to require a great deal of motivation before any improvement could be expected.

Richard was also looking at Clara. He was seeing her through Jim's eyes. Richard's thoughts danced back and forth in what must have been Jim's "movie" about Clara – how he felt during those years of friendship during high school, perhaps seeing her as the girl he could never have, and then discovering that destiny had allowed him to have her after all. Richard thought of those nights after she had actually said, "yes", when Jim planned how it would be with them growing old together. Then on those lonely days when he sat in that little rubber boat in that vast ocean and realized that he would never even see his Clara again – ever! The tears that Richard felt when he first read the message almost welled up again as he looked at Clara. He wondered if he was going to be able to read it today without breaking down completely.

Lastly, Clara, herself, felt that she was "looking at Clara". It was almost as if she were having some sort of "out of body" experience. It was as though she were looking on this scene and asking, "What is this message that this woman and this young man have in their possession? It has to be about Jim if it concerns Clara at all! Jim is the only concern that Clara has! Jim is Clara's life, pure and simple."

As they all sat expectantly, Richard reached into a small canvas bag and displayed a popular drink bottle with a cork in its opening. He explained the details of how he was fishing in one place and felt compelled to move over to one of the marker buoys, where he saw this little bottle floating and dancing in the foam. Then Richard brought out the message and said, "Clara, this message is primarily to you, but it has blessed my life and that of my mother and Betsey also. It is going to make you sad but I hope that it will bless your life too."

As Richard read the message, Gloria and Betsey were as touched as they were the very first time they heard it. They could not help but watch the results of each new word on Clara's face. There was a moment of unexpected joy when she realized that it was actually a message from her Jim. Then there was a wave of pain as it became evident that Jim was not going to survive. There were also times when it was evident that she was very proud of the things that he expressed and the obvious bravery that he was exhibiting in his final hours.

There were also vocal cues and lip biting and Clara's hands were very expressive. As you would expect, there were tears. But to Gloria's surprise, Clara did not really "break down"at any point during the message. There seemed to be a sense of acceptance, a shaking of the head in a "yes" motion as if to say, "this really confirms what I was afraid had happened." At the end she said, as if to herself and to nobody else, "Well, now I know. I finally know what happened! Thank God!"

After the message, when Gloria began to tell how she and Richard decided to share the message and to look for those who would benefit, Clara's face reflected deep appreciation and she repeated several times, "Thank you!", "Thank you!."

When Gloria told of the helpfulness of the secretary and the dedication of Sir Thomas, Clara's face and body language expressed deep appreciation and wonder that they would go to such extremes to offer help.

As Gloria and Richard finished all that they had to say, there was a brief silence, as if everyone had to take a few moments to "collect themselves" after this very emotional experience.

But then Clara raised her hand to indicate that she very much wanted to speak even though it was going to be difficult to speak at all because of her emotions.

Everyone looked at Clara and waited. "I want to thank you, Richard and Gloria, for your willingness to give of yourselves in this way. I want to thank Jim for being willing to use his last ounce of energy to carefully prepare a message that he did not really believe was going anywhere. I want to thank God for putting this loving plan into Jim's thoughts and then protecting and guiding that little bottle until it found its proper place and then leading

Richard to the very spot at the right time for him to find that little treasure. It was not the miracle that I prayed for but it was a miracle just the same. I must believe, because I trust God, that it was the miracle that I needed.

It is going to take time for my mind and my heart to work through all that I have heard and felt tonight. But, somehow I feel, in the midst of my deep sadness, that now I can live again. For all of these years I have been waiting to live "when Jim gets back!" Now, I must accept that he is not coming back. In some almost mysterious fashion I seem to have suddenly been given permission to live again. In an equally mysterious way I feel that Jim has reached out over those waters to tell me that he WANTS me to begin living again."

Gloria, Richard, and Betsey felt a sense of joy and relief that the message in the bottle had worked its miracle for Clara. They shook their heads in grateful wonder that this deep tragedy might actually turn into a positive outcome in Clara's life.

As they continued to talk, Clara suddenly said, "wait just a moment. There is something that I almost forgot and I am so glad it has come back to me now. When you were reading the message it crossed the back of my mind that there was something that you needed to know. I do not recognize the name of Bob Swithers, but I do know something of Melvin Dorster. Jim had said that Melvin had enlisted in Jamaica and that he was not exactly in the regular Royal Navy but was on loan from Jamaica for some kind of special project that was a joint effort between the British military and its Jamaican counterpart. I don't understand all about it but I just thought that if you have a problem finding anything on Melvin through Sir Thomas, you might find that there is someone in Jamaica that needs to hear this message as badly as I did.

Gloria said, "Oh Clara. If God had anything to do with us finding that little bottle in that big ocean – and I certainly believe He did, then I believe just as surely that he just brought that memory to you about Melvin Dorster. I would not be at all surprised if you have just given us our new assignment!"

Gloria, Richard, Clara, and Betsey talked long into the evening and finally exchanged many affectionate hugs and good wishes before saying good night. Gloria assured Clara that she and Richard would keep in touch with her and with her progress. They left their hand written copy of the original message with Clara and promised that they would have a photographic copy made for both Clara and Betsey.

Chapter 6. "A Day Of Rest".

When Gloria and Richard returned home on Saturday
evening, they were full of joy from what they had just
experienced with Betsey and Clara. They talked about it all
the way home. They were thrilled at the way Clara had
responded so positively and how the seeds of her "rebirth"
seemed to be appearing already.

Richard mentioned how amazingly the news about Melvin
Dorster had appeared. Gloria added, "If Clara had not
remembered to share the bit of information that Jim had
given her, we might never have known that Jamaica was
connected with Melvin. We would never have known
where to go to find out about Melvin. That would be
especially true if, for some reason Sir Thomas can not find
Melvin listed on the Royal Navy records.

When they got in the house they both had milk and
cookies, hugged each other, and said, "good night."

As Gloria and Richard rested in their beds, a strange thing
happened. Even though neither of them had mentioned it
to the other, they both thought of one obstacle that could
cause them some difficulty in the future.

For Richard it took this form: "Who would ever have
thought that this message might effect someone as far
away as Jamaica? I wonder how many miles away that is?
What would it cost to fly there and back, especially for two

of us? How could we possibly afford that? But there just isn't any way to present the message on the telephone or by mail! If we need to go to Jamaica, we will just have to find a way. Actually, we could use some of the money we have saved for my college!"

Gloria's thinking followed a similar pattern. "If there is someone living in Jamaica that was related to Melvin, then we will just have to find a way to get there. Not to share the message with his family or whoever it might be would be an absolute shame. It could be a wife or a mother just like me. We'll just have to use some of the money that Richard, Sr. left us 'for a rainy day'."

They both slept well after a day that had been both extremely stressful and, at the same time, very rewarding. They were both glad that tomorrow would be their "day of rest"!

Gloria and Richard woke up without the clock alarming. Sunday was a day of rest but it was also a day of worship for the Parsons family. Richard, Gloria, and her husband, Richard, Sr. – when he was living – did not have to think about what they were going to do on Sunday morning. Her husband's family were "church going folks" for three generations. Gloria was the daughter of a minister, so she had no choice as she grew up. Nor would she have made any other choice. She loved everything about her church experience. It was the center of her social life. In the small village where her father was Pastor, the friends at school were also her friends at church.

On this Sunday morning, Gloria prepared breakfast while Richard took his bath. After breakfast, Richard cleared the dishes while Gloria took her bath. That was their pattern on Sunday morning. In fact, that was their pattern for every part of their life together. Mother and Son worked together as two loving, considerate helpers. Richard had truly become the mature "man of the house" that his father had asked him to be.

At church that morning, the subject of the sermon was "You Have the Power to Bless". When the Pastor announced his title, Gloria looked over at Richard. They both smiled a knowing smile at each other. Almost everything the minister said related to the privilege that they felt God had given to them, at least where Jim and Clara were concerned and, hopefully where others related to Melvin Dorster and Bob Swithers were concerned also.

When Gloria and Richard got home from church, and while they were preparing lunch, they received a phone call from Clara. She sounded much more relaxed than she had seemed yesterday. She said that she had slept better than she had in years and wanted Gloria and Richard to know that she felt almost as though she had been reborn. She said, "It doesn't mean that I love Jim any less or that I don't still miss him very much, but knowing that he is safe and that there is no hope for his return allows me to be open, at least, to the possibility that there can still be joy and happiness in my future."

Then Clara said, "I have two, no three things, that I wanted to mention before I forget them. First, if you happen to find out the name of the secretary that was so helpful, I would like to be able to call her and just let her know what her extra efforts meant to me. Likewise, I would like to have a number where I could reach Sir Thomas. I have a strong need to let him hear my heart thank him. I think you probably feel the same way about him. And, lastly Gloria, it is strange that this one other fact came back to me this morning when I had forgotten it when I mentioned Melvin Dorster last night. I remembered that Melvin was, in fact, Dr. Melvin Dorster, and that he was a teacher of Political Science at some school in Jamaica. That might help you in some way later on."

"Oh, thank you so much, Clara, that actually gives us another approach to the 'Jamaica connection'. We can talk with Sir Thomas and ask him if he has found anything in the Royal Navy records and then we will have a place to begin in Jamaica also. I don't suppose you know the name of the school?"

"No, I'm sorry. Jim didn't know either"

"That's OK. We can find out later. We do want to find out about the secretary so that we can thank her too. We will write you a note with names and numbers for her and Sir Thomas. I can tell that you do feel better this afternoon, and I am so glad. Thank you for calling, Dear. Good bye!"

During lunch, Richard said, "You know, Mom, after lunch I think I will look in our Collier's Encyclopedia about schools in Jamaica. I think it was printed in 1951, so it should have some information about schools in that country."

"That is a great idea, Richard, and it wouldn't hurt for us to know more about Jamaica in general."

After lunch, Richard looked at the row of Collier's and found "I through K" in volume number 11. He found the article on Jamaica and was a little disappointed as he scanned and found no heading for Education. He read the first few sentences on "Topography and Climate" aloud to his mother. He skipped "Flora" He scanned "Population" and noted that it was made up of white, colored, black, East Indian, and Chinese. Of these, the black population outnumbered the others by far. He noted that Kingston is the capital.

He looked under "Government" and saw that Jamaica had been given a new constitution in 1944, which gave it more freedom of self government. He read, " 'It is headed by a Governor, assisted by the Privy Council, which advises the Governor in relation to the exercise of the Royal Prerogative, and the House of Representatives, consisting of 32 members'. But I don't see anything about 'Education'....Oh, here's something. 'There is a West Indian

Training School in Mandeville. It was established in 1936 and is seeking permission to become a two year college with the purpose of working toward a full University status. This could be it!"

"It sounds very promising!" said Gloria. "At the very least it is a good place to start! But that is about all we can do on our project today. I wouldn't want to bother Sir Thomas on his day of rest. But you know what I would very much like to do?"

"What is that, Mom?"
"I haven't been in your boat in a long time. Why don't we run over to Sandra and Carl's cottage at Brighton Beach and go for a little boat ride to just look out at that vast ocean and marvel at how that little bottle came to us!"

"I'm with you Mom. Let's do it!"

The Parsons family enjoyed the sea and had always been happy when they could spend some time on the water when times became stressful. They were at their boat in just a littlle over an hour. Gloria took her place on the stern bench and Richard faced her on the middle bench with the oars. He rowed out to the area where he had been fishing at the jetty. He said, "Mom, I was about here when I decided to go in. It was getting hot and I hadn't had even a nibble all afternoon. And then I spotted that marker buoy over there. I had such a strong urge to go over there that I do not think I could have done any other thing! It was not the idea that I might catch fish over there. It is hard to explain. It was just that I 'had to' go there! Of course, now we know why."

Richard rowed the short distance to the buoy and pointed to the very spot where he saw the bottle bobbing in the brown foam. "There's the spot, Mom. There is a little of that brown foam like I saw that day!"

They were both very quiet for a long time as they looked out into the beautiful ocean and thought about the many men who had lost their lives in its vastness during the war. "All those men", said Gloria, "may they rest in peace!"

Richard repeated her words as a toast, "Yes! May they rest in peace!"

Chapter 7. "A Door Opens".

At breakfast, on Monday morning, Richard said, "Mom, we really had a lot to happen over the weekend, but I guess we need to talk about where we go from here. It's only the middle of July, so I am free for about seven or eight weeks before school starts. But can you get off some from your real estate office?"

"That is the good thing about real estate, Richard. It goes on even when you are out of town. I have some closings scheduled that I can work around, and in a pinch someone else can cover for me. I have some homes listed that other salesmen can show. So, within reason I will have no difficulty getting the time off that we will need."

"Then, what is our next step?"

"Well, I will call Sir Thomas when I get to the office and see if he has found anything in his records for Melvin or Bob. I will also give him my office phone number so he can reach me either there or at home. If you are at home around noon, I will call you and let you know if I have heard anything."

When Gloria got to the office at 9:30 there was a message waiting for her. "A Sir Thomas Lawn called and asked that you call his office."

Gloria was excited and puzzled at the same time and could

hardly wait to call him. She was chagrined that the Broker had called a sales meeting for 9:45 and she was "on pins and needles" during the whole rather boring procedure. It was 11:00 before she was free to make her call.

When she called Sir Thomas' private number, he answered immediately. "Hello, Sir Thomas, this is Gloria Parsons. I would have called sooner but this was my first free moment."

"Oh, yes, Mrs. Parsons. How good of you to return my call. I called your home earlier and your son gave me your office number. I hope that was all right."

"Sir Thomas, I will appreciate your calling either number at any time that you have any new information for us. Thank you for calling today!"

"Good! To get right to the point, I have learned a few things that were quite surprising. I did find Melvin Dorster's name in our records and there was a rather lengthy bit of information – much more than we would have on an ordinary sailor."

"It seems that he was no ordinary sailor. He was in the Royal Navy by very special arrangement between our government and the chaps in Kingston, Jamaica. He was given a temporary rank in the Navy and a special clearance that would allow him to pass rather freely through our military and government "red tape". He could fly on our planes and sail on our ships in order to orient himself to the flavor of our navy life."

"It seems that we were building a ship, a cruiser, in honor of our long relationship with Jamaica. The HMS Jamaica was to have been commissioned in May of 1942 – just two months after Melvin Dorster died at sea. Of course, the records did not know that he had died. He was listed as 'missing in action'. Part of my surprise was that he was not Mr. Dorster but Dr. Dorster! He was apparently a teacher of Political Science somewhere in Jamaica."

Gloria interrupted Sir Thomas. "Sir Thomas, Clara told us that Jim had told her of a Melvin Dorster and that he was actually a Dr. Dorster and had taught at some school in Jamaica. So your information confirms that!"

"How interesting! It seems that someone in charge of the festivities of the commissioning of the HMS Jamaica thought it would be a good idea to have someone to represent Jamaica at that commissioning. - someone who had a good handle on not only British history but on Jamaican history as well. Dr. Dorster was scheduled as the main speaker for that event and as a result of his experiences with the Navy he could speak more personally about life on a Royal Navy ship. But, unfortunately his ship was sunk by the German sub before the event took place."

"That is so amazing, Sir Thomas. That information helps a

great deal. Was there any information about where Dr. Dorster taught or of any family connections?"

"That was not included, Gloria. It did give his home town as Mandeville in Jamaica."

"Oh, Sir Thomas, that fits in! We were looking in Colliers' Encyclopedia and it did say that there is a school of higher learning in Mandeville. It is the West Indian Training School. It has been trying to reach Junior college status, so perhaps they could have had a person of Dr. Dorster's standing on their faculty. I will call that facility by phone tomorrow, and find out any information I can about Dr. Dorster. I will also look into what sort of connections I can make from London to Jamaica by air."

"You mean that you are actually considering going to Jamaica yourself? Can you take away from your work?"

"Sir Thomas, this is too important to let it drop at this point. I just have to follow through with this. And I must take Richard with me. It means every bit as much to him as it does to me, perhaps more."

"Well, both of you have shown a splendid sense of humanity, Gloria. Whether you realize it or not, there is a great deal of patriotism wrapped up in what you are doing. England has a stake in what you are trying to accomplish. After all, Dr. Dorster came here at the request of the Royal Navy. I believe we owe something to Jamaica and to any family and friends who might still be there. Let me say this. Please do not finalize any travel plans just yet. Give me a little time. There are some avenues at my disposal that I would like to explore."

"Thank you, Sir Thomas. I really do not know what we would have done without your help!"

"It is my deep pleasure, Gloria. You and Richard have had a very rare privilege entrusted to you and you are carrying it beautifully. I am just glad to have a part in it. I will get back as soon as I have further news."

"Thank you, Sir Thomas."

When Gloria came home at 5:30, Richard was radiant. "You look like the cat that ate the canary", quipped Gloria."

"Sir Thomas called about five minutes ago. He said he thought that you would be home already and that he would call a little later with some good news."

"OK. Well, I see that you have some chops on the range. What would you like with them, spinach and potatoes or peas and sweet yams?"

"Yes to all of the above!"

"You mouse! It's either or!"

"OK. Peas and yams it is!"

As they sat down for their meal, the phone rang. "Hello, Gloria, Thomas Lawn here!"

"We were hoping it would be you!"

"Are you eating dinner?"

"Yes, but barely. It is far more nourishing to both of us to talk with you, Sir Thomas, than anything we could possibly be eating for dinner."

"You are spoiling me, pure and simple! Well, here's what I've got and I think you will like it. The Navy has an arrangement with the Royal Air Force and they have a round trip to Jamaica each week. It takes about 22 hours each way, with stops at the Azores, Bermuda, and another location I am not familiar with. They leave London each Wednesday morning at about 6:00 A.M. And get to Jamaica at about 4:00 in the morning. Then they lay over for 24 hours in Jamaica and leave there on Friday morning for the return trip. Do you think you are up for that?"

"Oh, yes! By all means!"

"They use the flight for pilot and navigator training and as a courier service for government business. They usually use a DC 4, which is not as fast as the new jet plane service offered by 'the Comet' and is not 'non stop' like the Comet, but it has proved to be very safe and dependable. They usually have one or two military or governmental passengers. It is rather unorthodox for them to allow civilian passengers, but they are willing to make an exception in your case, due to the unusual nature of your mission."

"You have the option of coming back on the same round trip if your business can be completed in 24 hours or you can stay over – if your time permits – until the return flight on the following Friday. Now, this would be totally without charge to you and Richard. You would only be responsible for your food and lodging while on the trip. How does that sound to you?"

Gloria paused for a moment and took a deep breath. Then she replied, "I am utterly overwhelmed, Sir Thomas. I am totally speechless. We knew that we must go to Jamaica and make an attempt, at least, to find someone who was related in some way to Dr. Dorster. But how we would afford such a venture was still in the form of a dream.

Your offer certainly opens the doors to our dream. Richard is entirely free at this time and I can make arrangements rather easily to take a few days off. Would it be possible to go this Wednesday, that is, the day after tomorrow?"

"Gloria, it sounds to me that you are extremely flexible and it is my understanding that you simply need to show up about 30 minutes ahead of time so that you can sign several permission and information forms. That's all. It will be the same coming back. Show up for the first return flight or wait a week."

"Let me say 'thank you so much', Sir Thomas, for arranging this for us. My first thought about this is 'the sooner, the better'. I would like for us to take the plane this Wednesday if that is OK. Would you please give me the address of the airport?"

"Actually, Gloria, if you don't mind, I would like to pick you and Richard up and take you to the airport in my car, for two reasons. First, the location is just a little obscure if you are not familiar with the area. I would also like to be able to introduce you to the people involved. Secondly, I have been looking forward to meeting you both ever since our lives first "crossed'. Will that be acceptable to you? I have already taken the liberty of looking up your address in the telephone listings."

"I think that would be wonderful. I really hate for you to be up at that early hour. I understand that the departure time is 6:00 A.M., and we are to be there 30 minutes before that. That's 5:30. So would you set the time for us to be ready?"

"Gloria, I really hate to tell you, but to be sure that the traffic does not hold us up I would say that 4:30 would be a safe time. I really apologize for that!"

"Sir Thomas, I have left home many times at 4:30 in the morning just to go fishing and this is vastly more important than any fishing trip. It is absolutely no problem for me or Richard. We will be ready with 'bells on' ".

"Good show! Spoken like a trooper! So, 4:30 it is. I will be in a 1950 blue English Ford. Just to be absolutely sure, you are at 57 Ramshead Place, correct?"

"You are exactly right, Sir Thomas!" Gloria said the last statement with a definite 'smile in her voice' as if to say, ' you are an amazing man indeed!'"

"And, Gloria, would you mind it very much if I asked you to please call me Thom?"

"Then 'Thom' it is for me. But still 'Sir Thomas' for Richard, if you don't mind."

"Agreed, Gloria. And 'til then!"

"Until then, Thom!"

Gloria thought to herself, "He is such a nice man! 'Thom', yes, I like that better. I wonder how old he is."

Chapter 8. "Getting Ready".

Gloria woke up on Tuesday morning with great excitement. She had so much to do before tomorrow, but her "juices" were flowing. She had boundless energy. She figured she would have plenty of time to rest on the plane if she wore herself out at a rapid pace today.

After the usual breakfast routine, Gloria selected two groups of clothes – those that she would wear if the short trip of three days was sufficient. She then added several "low maintenance " items in case the trip had to be extended until the next Friday. She selected "fast dry" items that could be washed in a bath room and hung to dry on the shower rod. She helped Richard to do the same with his clothes.

She had a few minutes before she had to leave for work, so she went back to the Colliers' Encyclopedia, Volume 11, and opened again to Jamaica. She scanned the History section and saw that the Spanish had dominated the country at first and then the English came in. She found that the aborigines had largely died off and had been replaced by slaves that came in with the slave trade. Finally came the abolition of slavery, but not before an independent slave culture had developed. The country had been devastated time after time by hurricanes and earth quakes. The whole picture boggled her mind. She envisioned that she and Richard were about to experience a cultural shock like they had never before seen in their protected London environment.

When Gloria pulled up in front of her office, she was relieved to see that Sam's car was already there. Sam was her Broker/Boss and she really needed to talk with him. She knocked on his door and asked if he had a few minutes. Sam Daughtry welcomed her warmly. "I always have time for you, Gloria!" She knew that he meant that sincerely and he had never failed to show it.

She pulled up a chair and said, "Sam, I need to be gone at least for the rest of this week – and maybe even through Friday of next week. I won't know for sure until this Friday. Now, before you respond, let me tell you the reason for my absence."

"Please do, Gloria. It has to be a good reason because you just never leave London."

Sam sat back and listened as Gloria told him the whole story from the beginning until the very present. When she was finished, Sam grinned and his pride in Gloria was as obvious as if she had been his own daughter. "This is a marvelous thing that you are doing and if there is any way at all that I can help you can count on me to do it. Now, do you want this to be kept between us at this point or can I share it with the others?"

"If you don't mind, Sam, I would like for you not to mention it while I am here, simply because I have so much to do before this evening that I just don't have a minute to talk with anyone about it today."

"I understand, Gloria. Is there anything I can do at this point to help?"

"Only this, Sam. I need to make at least one, maybe two, long distance phone calls to Jamaica. I would appreciate it if I could call from here with the understanding that I will pay the charges when the bill comes in."

"I have no problem with that, Gloria. Don't hesitate to make all of the calls you need."

"Thanks, Sam."

Gloria went to her office, checked her mail, and saw that she had no messages waiting for her attention. She made a brief list of what she needed to do"

1.Call the international operator.

2.Get a phone number for the West Indian Training School in Mandeville.

3.Dial the school and see where that leads

As Gloria sat there, looking at her list, she rehearsed what she would say. "Should I begin by asking if I could speak to someone who had been there a dozen years since Dr.

Dorster's death? Should I just begin by asking if the name, Dr. Melvin Dorster is familiar to the person who answers the phone?"

She decided to dial the number, if she is able to get such a number, and just follow her instincts.

She did get the international operator , who said, "I will be glad to get Jamaica for you, Mrs. Parsons. It sometimes takes a while to set it up with the present transatlantic cable system and the connections are not always too clear. But I will be happy to make the connections for you. Would you like for me to set up the call for you now, Mrs. Parsons?"

"I think so, but first, do you have any way of knowing what the time would be in Jamaica now?"

"Why, yes, the time there would be exactly 5:00 A.M., Ma'am. They are six hours earlier than London in the summer and five hours earlier in the winter months. If you would like for me to wait until a certain time to make the call for you, I will be glad to make a note of that and call you back at that time."

"Oh, you can do that? That would be marvelous! Let me see, if I say 9:00 A.M. in Jamaica, that would be..?"

"That would be 3:00 in London, Ma'am."

"Then that would work fine. So, please call me back at 3:00 at this number. Ask for Gloria Parsons. I will appreciate it!"

"I will be more than happy to do that, Ma'am."

Gloria decided that, since it was already 11:00, she would call Richard and tell him she would stop by and get some fish and chips for both of them and be home at noon. Then she would go by a pharmacy and get a few items that they might need for the trip.

Gloria and Richard enjoyed their lunch and she washed out a few things. Richard got their luggage down from the attic while his mother hung out the the laundry to dry.

Gloria was back at the office by 2:00, with just enough time to make several phone calls to assure that her responsibilities were taken care of for a week and a half if necessary.

At exactly 3:00 her phone rang. It was the international operator. "Mrs. Gloria Parsons?"

"This is she."

"I can set up your call now if you are ready."

"Yes, I am ready, thank you!"

"Please hang up and stay by the phone. I will make the necessary connections and call you back when I have the

Jamaica call ready. So, I believe you said that you want the West Indian Training School, in Mandeville, Jamaica. Is that correct?"
"Yes, thank you."

In a few minutes the operator rang again and said, "Mrs. Parsons, I have the secretary at the school on the line. Is that satisfactory?"

"Oh yes!" answered Gloria"

"Then go ahead with your conversation, Mrs. Parsons."

"Hello. This is Mrs. Gloria Parsons in U.K.."

"Yes, Mrs. Parsons. This is the West Indian Training School. How may I be of service?" The woman had a bright, cheery voice. Gloria was so glad that she did not have any trouble understanding her.

Gloria decided to begin with the name. "Yes, thank you. I am seeking anyone who might recognize the name of Dr. Melvin Dorster."

There was a long pause.

"Are you still there?", said Gloria.

"Is this a joke, Ma'am?"

"No. I am very serious. Why would you think that I am joking?"

"Because, Ma'am, in Jamaica, asking if we recognize the name of Dr. Melvin Dorster is like asking you if you recognize the name of Winston Churchill."

"Oh, my. Oh, no. I mean, I didn't know! Then, please let me start over. I do feel very foolish. Was Dr. Dorster affiliated at one time with your school?"

"Yes Ma'am. He was one of several teachers who banded together to raise the level of our academic standards. It was Dr. Dorster who first voiced the hope that we would some day be a first rate University. Any student that enters our school learns how important Dr. Dorster was to not only the school but to all of Jamaica."

"Did you know Dr. Dorster personally?"

"No Ma'am. I was just a little girl when Dr. Dorster became missing."

"Do you know of anyone at the school now that knew him personally?"

There was another pause. "Yes, Ma'am."

"Could you give me the name and, perhaps, a telephone number?"

"There are many who knew him well. Many! But perhaps your best person for that purpose would be his own brother, Dr. Leitman Dorster. He should be at the school now if he is not on other business elsewhere. I will switch you to his telephone."

"Oh, thank you so much. you have been most helpful. Could I have your name?"

"I am Nita Costanza, and thank you. I will switch you now."

Gloria was amazed that her very first contact might be the brother of Melvin Dorster.

She hears a phone ringing and then, "Hello, this is West Indian Training School, Dr. Dorster's office." Gloria was nervous at the prospect of what she was about to do.

"Yes, this is Mrs. Gloria Parsons in London. I would like to speak with Dr. Leitman Dorster if he is available."

"Dr. Dorster is gone for the day. I am his secretary. May I be of assistance?"

"Yes, thank you. I plan to be in Jamaica on Thursday, the day after tomorrow, for just one day. Is there any chance that I could have an appointment with Dr. Dorster? The earlier, the better."

"Yes, he should be here on Thursday morning. He is taking a group of students on a short trip later in the day. We can give you an appointment at 9:00 A.M. if that is satisfactory."

"That would be wonderful. There will be two of us. My son, Richard, will be with me."

"May I tell Dr. Dorster the nature of your appointment?'

"If you would, just say that I have some information concerning his brother, Dr. Melvin Dorster."

"Oh, my! Anything about his brother is going to be greatly appreciated, I assure you! Thank you! I am sure he will be anxious to talk with you. Now, again, your name is...?"

"Gloria Parsons, and my son, Richard. We are from London, U.K".

"Thank you so much. I will let him know as soon as possible, Mrs. Parsons. Is that all?"

"Yes, thank you, and good bye."

Gloria was feeling "on top of the world!" Who would have believed that she could already have an appointment with Dr. Dorster's brother? She thought, "Now, what else do I need to do before we leave? I should have made a check list! Oh, I do need to call Clara and give her my news."

Then she remembered that she had not checked on the name of the secretary that had been so helpful. She looked up the original Royal Navy telephone number and dialed. She was almost sure that the same young woman answered as before, but she briefly reviewed their former conversation and the young woman said, "Oh, yes Mum. I do remember our conversation!"

"Then I want to thank you from the bottom of my heart for your help. If you had given up without finding Sir Thomas, then this whole project might have died from the start. There is another person who benefited greatly from your efforts. Her name is Clara Woolsey. Would you mind if I give her your name and number?"

"Oh, No Mum. I won't mind at all. I am Beth Ambrose and you already have my number."

"Thank you so much, Beth, and my son, Richard, thanks you also!"

Gloria then called Clara Woolsey. She intended to just give her the information about Beth and Sir Thomas, but she could not possibly keep her new developments from Clara. She told her about her free flight to Jamaica and about what she had learned so far about Dr. Melvin Dorster. She told in detail how she contacted the school and about her pending appointment with Dr. Dorster's brother on Thursday morning. Even at that she was much more brief than she desired to be.

The rest of the day consisted of dinner, last minute preparations, setting the alarm clock for 3:30, and a very early bed time!

Chapter 9. "Meeting Sir Thomas"

Gloria had a difficult time going to sleep on Tuesday evening. She turned out the lights at 9:00. She typically went to bed about 10:30. She realized she was smiling. She was remembering the old poem about Christmas in which "visions of sugar plums danced in their heads!" and she thought of all that was dancing in her head as she tried to quiet her thoughts. There was the fear of not waking up with the clock, anxiety about making a good impression on Sir Thomas ("I wonder where that popped up from", she thought), concern about the safety of flying in the DC 4 ("those old planes were flown in the war, weren't they?"). Then she switched to thoughts of Jamaica, and that took her through another 30 minutes of imagining. She finally got up at about 10:30 and tip toed into Richard's room. Thankfully he was visibly in deep slumber. This eased her mind a bit and she was asleep soon after getting back in bed.

She did wake easily with the clock. Since they were going to have a quick breakfast, she took her shower first to give Richard a few extra minutes of sleep. Then she called him for his bath and she boiled the porridge (rolled oats) and prepared the coffee.

They usually ate a typical English "fry up", which consisted of eggs and sausage (or bacon), fried bread, baked beans, mushrooms, and coffee. But Gloria was just a bit afraid of how such a breakfast might work aboard a

A Message For All Time

long flight to Jamaica, especially if it got "bumpy".

While she waited for the oats to boil, she prepared
sandwiches for their lunch. She had no idea what the usual
lunch procedure was on such a flight. Would the crew
members have their own bag? Would one of their stops
coincide with lunch time? So she decided to fix two
sandwiches for each, including a four man crew. She fixed
tuna and mayonnaise for one and ham and pickles for the
other. all on some home made wheat bread. She included
some apples, bananas, and chips to fill out the lunch. She
was surprised at the size of the bag required to hold the
whole lot. It looked like she had just come from the grocer.

By the time she had finished her oats, she had only twenty
minutes to get ready. She found her self annoyed because
she would have little time to arrange her hair and make up.
"Why am I so concerned about looking good?" she
wondered. "Who am I trying to impress?" In the back of
her mind she knew that there was a part of her somewhere
that wanted to impress this man whose voice and manner
were so kind and whose face she had begun to try to form
in her mind's eye.

At precisely 4:30, there was a knock on the door. Gloria
found her self thinking that "even his knock sounds kind
and considerate!" She laughed at her own "craziness."
She opened the door and, for a brief moment, betrayed her
own surprise. She had expected to see someone who
looked like the actor, Monty Woolley. Instead, there was a

man who rivaled the looks of Sir Laurance Olivier, Peter O'Toole, and Richard Burton.

"Mrs. Parsons?"

"Sir Thomas? Well, of course you are Sir Thomas. Who else would be ringing my door bell at 4:30 in the morning?" (To herself - "I am sounding like a babbling idiot! What is wrong with me?")

"Have you forgotten our agreement? I am Thom, remember?"
"Thom, of course, and this is my son, Richard."

"I am so glad to meet you, Sir Thomas!" Richard's smile is partly his friendliness to Sir Thomas, but it is also partly from his amusement at his mother's obvious befuddlement at the sight of Sir Thomas.

"I am so pleased to finally meet you, Richard!"

"I would invite you in, Thom, but we are ready if you are."

"Yes, I guess we had better be going."

Thom lifted the small boot (trunk) lid of his little English Ford and everything fit in nicely. He then opened the front door for Gloria and the back door for Richard. Richard had to angle his legs a bit to fit his six foot frame into the somewhat small but comfortable rear seat.

"I am sorry about the small space, Richard."

"Sir Thomas, I love the English Ford. I have always admired this car. It would be my choice if I were shopping for a car. I am very comfortable, really!"

"Thanks, Richard. You are either very kind or a born diplomat!"

"I would say that I am honest, Sir."

Gloria was just a little uneasy with that little "give and take." Was Richard miffed? Would Thom take his reply as a rebuff?

"Well said", Richard, "Said as a man!"

Richard swelled with pride and felt admiration for Sir Thomas.

Gloria felt relieved and proud of her son. He was becoming a man! She held her lunch bag in her lap and mentioned that she was not sure of the usual lunch provisions on a flight of this nature, so she thought she would err on the side of abundance. Sir Thomas agreed with her thinking.

Thom started the engine and Gloria gave him time to get on the road. She had wanted to know more about Sir Thomas' military experience and began by saying, "I believe you said that you were in the Royal Navy?"

"Yes, Gloria. I went into the Navy in 1934, soon after graduation from high school. My father was a house painter and very good at it. He had done that all of his life. He had made a successful business and wanted me to follow in his foot steps. Well, I tried it for a year and could not stand it! I think I joined the Navy as the only honorable way that I could see to leave the painting business without breaking my Dad's heart."

"So I went in as an ordinary seaman and was privileged to be assigned to an area that was sort of the "diplomatic wing" of the Navy. I had to learn the 'ins and outs ' of diplomacy just to survive. I spent 15 years in the Navy in a life that I loved. I am sure that I would have stayed longer but one of my fellow officers was offered a job in government that he could not refuse and he talked me into retiring to be his assistant. So that is how I wound up in a very satisfying position and how I had the 'Sir' attached to my name. I am always a bit embarrassed by that but I do feel deeply honored that it was given."

"Now, I have talked far too much! Please tell me about you and Richard!"

"There isn't much to tell, really. My husband, Richard Sr., was my high school sweet heart. When we graduated in 1935, I got a job at a dime store just to save up some money for us to get married. Richard went to work in his father's hardware store. By 1936 we were married. We had to live with his parents during that first year until we could rent our own place. Richard Jr. was born the next year. We had our little 'love nest' and thought 'All is right with the world'."

"Then, when things began to go awful in 1939, Richard joined the Royal Navy. He was on a destroyer and really enjoyed that. He came home whenever he got the chance. Then, in 1943, his ship was torpedoed. His leg was damaged and he had to have an amputation as a result. He was given a medical discharge. He came home and took over his father's hardware store. For eight years we had what you might call an ideal family. We were very happy. But three years ago Richard Sr. had an unexpected complication from the amputation and he died, almost over night. Richard Jr. and I were, of course, devastated."

"I am sorry", said Thom. "I am, indeed, sorry. I also know that sorrow. My Lois died five years ago, quite without warning. I woke up one morning and she had died quietly during the night. I had not heard a cry or anything. They said that it was from a heart problem that she had probably had all of her life but it had never been detected."

"Well, it would seem that we have the Navy and personal loss in common, Thom. Do you have any children?"

"Our commonality stops there, Gloria. Lois and I always wanted children but we never enjoyed that blessing. I find myself silently envying folks, like yourself, who have a son."

"We are almost there. The Air Port is over to the right. We will be checked at the gate and I am sure they are expecting us. I really wish I were going with you. I believe this is going to be a wonderful experience for both of you. I have not had a chance to talk with you, Richard, and I really look forward to that opportunity in the future, I hope.

"I sincerely hope so too, Sir!"

Gloria found herself very proud of Richard's mature response.

Then she surprised herself by placing her hand on Thom's hand as she said, "Thom, I really can not tell you how much this means to Richard and me. You have leveled the road for us, and I really do thank you." She continued to look into his eyes and wanted to say more, but thought better of it.

"I will stay with your project to the very end and will do all that I can to help. I am almost as deeply involved in the outcome as you are, if that is possible."

Thom went around the car and opened the door for Gloria and then for Richard. He opened the boot and grabbed one of the cases as Richard took the other. Gloria brought her arm load of food.

The guards at the gate gave a smart salute, showing their respect for this retired Navy officer. Then they gave a friendly greeting to Gloria and Richard. Gloria wondered if these men had been briefed as to the nature of their being there. The DC4 was already warming up just around the corner from the gate and, after signing several forms, they were allowed to go directly aboard.

Thom allowed Gloria and Richard to go on first. The pilot and co pilot were in their seats and there were two other men at what Gloria assumed was a radio/navigation table on the right side of the cockpit.

"Gentlemen, I would like for you to meet two of my favorite people. This is Mrs. Gloria Parsons and her son, Richard. I have met the Pilot. Gloria and Richard, this is Pilot Officer Harold Fontain. I will let him introduce the others."

The pilot got out of his seat in order to introduce the other three men.

"Thank you, Sir Thomas. Gloria, Richard, and Sir Thomas, this is AirCraftsman Joel Kitchens, who is on the last leg of his Pilot training. This is Chief Technician Charles "Chuck" Craft, who is a Navigations Instructor. With him is AirCraftsman Dennis Huff, who is finalizing his navigation rank but I assure you that, if anything should happen to myself or Chuck, Heaven forbid, these other two gentlemen could get you there quite safely."

"Well, I will depart with great sorrow that I can not enjoy the ride with you. If you don't mind, Gloria, would you please call me some time tomorrow and reverse the charges. Let me know how things are going and if you will be coming on back or staying another week. Do you have my number with you?"

"Yes, I do, eh Sir Thomas." They exchange a knowing smile that she has just added the "Sir" out of respect and for the benefit of the men. "And thank you again for all of your help!"

Chapter 10. "Remembering".

"Now, Mrs. Parsons, let me stow this package. Is this your lunch?"

"Yes. I wasn't sure of how you did lunch on a flight. So I brought some sandwiches."

"We don't have any special way. What usually happens is that we get to our first stop in the Azores at about 2:00 this afternoon. So we usually eat our lunch. Then the next hop is 9 hours to Bermuda, but that puts us there in Bermuda at about 11. That is pretty late to eat and we sometimes just get a cup of coffee and a roll at a little all night counter there. What I would suggest is that we eat lunch in the airport in the Azores - they have some good lunch shops there, and then you could save your sandwiches for your regular dinner time at 6:00 or whatever. How does that sound? "

"That sounds wonderful and I made enough for everybody"

"That will be great."

"Thank you, Pilot Officer Fontain"

"Could we go with first names? Is that OK with you? Especially where the crew is concerned. That would make it easier on us, if you would not consider that a lack of respect"

"Agreed! So, Harold, Joel, Chuck, and Dennis. Me, Gloria." Gloria did an impromptu imitation of Tarzan and they both laughed.

"You are very good to have the names down already!"

"I am in real estate so I have to catch names the first time around."

"Now, you do understand the time frame? It is a 22 hour trip, with stops in the Azores, Bermuda, Nassau, and then Kingston. The extra stops are necessary because of the somewhat limited range of these DC4's. But they are very dependable."

"Now, let's have a quick seat belt check to be sure you know how to buckle and unbuckle. Now, if you will look under your seat, you will see a life preserver. They are just like you would use on a cruise. They inflate by pulling the little lanyard on your chest. Do that only after you have put the vest on. We are going to be over the ocean most of the way so do take the life vest seriously. We do have rubber dingies too but these vests will hold you up almost indefinitely."

"Now, please buckle your seat belts and keep them buckled until I tell you it is safe to unbuckle. Then you may move about carefully within the plane. You are welcome to visit the cockpit if you wish to watch at any time, and if we are not too busy we will be delighted to chat. Good to have you with us!"

Gloria sat on the aisle seat and Richard sat next to the window. As they took off, Gloria held Richard's hand and they smiled at each other. Neither had mentioned to anyone that this was the first time they had ever been in an airplane. They were just a little bit anxious! Well, actually a lot anxious! But their mission was worth it.

After they were in the air and everything checked out, Harold said, "It is now safe to release your seat belts. If we get into any rough weather it might be necessary to fasten your belts again, but I will let you know if that is the case. Now, if you will look out your window to the right, you can wave 'good bye' to 'Dear old England'!"

Richard decided that he would try to pick up where he left off when the clock rang at 3:30. He found the knob that let his seat fall back into a resting position.

Gloria wanted to just relax and enjoy the moderate quietness of the cabin. So much had happened during the last few days. This was the first time she could relax without feeling that she needed to be doing something. Her mind went back to this morning and the first time that she had actually seen Thom. What a surprise! Such a charming man! He was actually quite different from Richard, her husband.

Richard would never have inspired her to use the word, "charming". Gloria loved her husband dearly, but he certainly had his short comings. He was not good looking. He was shorter than she and a bit obese after he came back from the war. He was often moody and seldom showed much concern for her feelings. But he was faithful and dependable. In spite of his lack of outward affection, she knew that he loved her deeply. He was a good father to Richard, and taught him so much about being a strong and dependable man.

They had been happy together. But after Richard's death she had gone to real estate school and had found satisfaction in her work. She had never considered the need for remarriage. She had never seen a man who aroused anything more than friendship since Richard's death.

Still, she had to admit that Thom had caused feelings that she had not felt since her days in high school. She had actually looked forward to meeting him in person. Then, to her surprise, she actually hated to see him get off of the plane this morning!

As Gloria thought about Thom, she relaxed in her seat and eased her seat back down a little. She began to count the good qualities she had already noticed about him – his good looks, his soft voice, his considerate ways. It was like 'counting sheep' in a way. She went to sleep with a smile on her face.

After an hour into the flight, Richard awoke with a start. He had forgotten where he was. He looked over at his mother and saw that she was sleeping soundly. He began to think of the many events since he had found the message.

As he thought of the sailors in that little rubber boat, his memory went to his father and the mixture of feelings that surrounded his relationship with him. He loved his father and he missed him sorely. He realized that there was some resentment there, however. It was as though he blamed his father for those years in the Navy and the years since he died – years when most boys enjoyed learning so much from their dads. He felt that it was unfair for him not to have a father to look up to now. It was unfair for his mother to have to spend the rest of her life alone – especially after he goes out into the world to find his own future.

Then he thought about how life deals so strangely with people. There is Sir Thomas – a wonderful man who would probably be a great father and who wanted a child all of his adult life, and yet, never had one. Here I am without a father, and I really need one. Richard realized that, for the third time in a week, tears were cascading down his cheeks.

As Gloria and Richard flew toward Jamaica, Clara Woolsey had spent her morning going through the box of letters that she had received from Jim. It was part of the process of adjusting her life to the new reality of his death. She was suddenly stunned by a paragraph in a letter that she had received just shortly before he disappeared. This is what she read: "Clara, do you remember that I mentioned a sailor that is actually a college professor, in civilian life? His name is Dr. Melvin Dorster. Well, they got him in the Navy mainly because he is going to represent Jamaica when we christen the new cruiser, HMS Jamaica in May of this year. He is to be the Dedicatory Speaker. His bunk is right under mine and last night he was quietly rehearsing his speech but I was able to hear every word. Something he said really stuck in my mind and I wanted to pass it on to you before I forget it because to me it is really special. Listen to this. It is almost word for word as he said it.

'It has been a profound gift to me, as a citizen of Jamaica, to have had the privilege of knowing the young men who are serving so bravely in this war. I think of their courage and their sincere devotion to country, to God, and to truth. But this war will not last forever. These young men and those young women who are showing their courage back home even now – they will need to find schools that are worthy of nourishing their good minds, schools that will receive them with open arms.'

'I, for one, have been given a new vision of the need for those schools to have the very highest of standards and goals. As a person who has some influence in such a school, I plan to go back to the country for which this fine ship is named, and help to establish one of the finest universities in the Western Hemisphere. With God's help and the help of my fellow countrymen, it WILL happen!' "

When Clara read this speech, she was overwhelmed by remorse. "Oh, God. How did I forget this when I was talking with Gloria. She is going to speak with the brother of this great man, and I am the only person in this whole world who has knowledge of this speech that Dr. Dorster never had the opportunity to deliver! These words could properly be carved on the cornerstone of the new university. But first they need to be heard by those who can still make that university a reality! I must get this speech to Gloria. But how?"

Clara thought about how Sir Thomas had arranged for the flight to Jamaica. "Perhaps he has a phone number or an address where I can send it before Gloria has her appointment with Dr. Dorster's brother", she thought.. "Yes, here is Sir Thomas' phone number. Perhaps he will have a suggestion."

Clara dialed the number and Sir Thomas answered. "Is this Sir Thomas Lawn?"

"Yes, it is."

"This is Clara Woolsey, I..."

"Yes, Mrs. Woolsey. I am so glad you called. I have heard so much from Gloria Parsons about you! Oh, please excuse my bad manners. I was so excited when you said your name that I did not listen to what you were going to tell me. I am sorry."

"That is quite all right, Sir Thomas. Gloria gave me your number yesterday so that I could thank you for all that you have done for me – for all of us. You have literally given me back my life. We have not seen the end of what that message from those men will do to benefit many others. Surely God is behind this whole thing in some way!"

"I am as grateful as you are, Dear Lady, and I certainly agree that this has been an act of God."

"Now that I have said that, Sir Thomas, I have something of a rather urgent nature to share with you." Clara then read what Jim had said in the letter, including the whole speech.

"Thank you so much for calling me about this, Clara. There really is no way for us to imagine how far reaching this speech may be. It could become the beginning of a new movement toward the goal of a university in Jamaica. It is, as you sensed, important that this reach Gloria while she is in Jamaica. It seems to me that the timing is also important. If Gloria can have this before she goes for her appointment tomorrow morning, she will have so much more than she would have had in simply confirming Dr. Dorster's death. She will be raising his voice and his purpose beyond the limitations imposed by his death."

"Do you have time to dictate, word for word, what you have just read? If so, I have pen and paper here and will take it down as you speak."
"Yes! Yes! I am ready!"

"I will write this all down. I know that she is going to call me some time tomorrow, so we are guaranteed that she will have this while she can still relay it to Dr. Dorster's brother. But I will make every effort to get it to her before that appointment. Thank you again, Clara. I will keep you informed about what I find out."

"Thank you, Sir Thomas."
"Thom made a telephone call to confirm a possibility that he had in mind. He found out that it would be quite easy to send the message to Gloria aboard the plane. He went immediately to the Air Port where they had been earlier in the day. They put him directly in touch with the navigator aboard the plane. He dictated the entire message to the navigator and then asked if it would be permissible for him to speak briefly to Mrs. Parsons. The navigator said that it would be fine and went to get Gloria.

"Yes, this is Gloria!"

"Gloria, I would not have done this unless it were important and you will see how very important it was that I call." Then Thom related all that Clara had said to him, including the speech.

"Oh, Thom. You DO know how very important this news will be to everyone concerned. Surely God has had a hand in this whole event from the beginning. There could not possibly have been this many simple coincidences without Divine intervention!"

"That is exactly what Clara said", replied Thom.

"I know we should not speak too long, Thom. Thank you again!"

"I will talk with you again tomorrow, Gloria. This might sound inappropriate, but I miss you ..and Richard, already."

"Me too, Thom!"

Gloria went back to her seat to share the good news with Richard, who was already sitting on the front of his seat in expectation.

Gloria could not help but pause for a moment, before starting her story for Richard, to enjoy Thom's closing words, "I miss you...already."

Chapter 11: "Another Good Bye".

Gloria told Richard what had happened and showed him the copy of the message that the navigator had written down before calling her to the radio.

Richard read the speech and shook his head in amazement. "This is almost like discovering a message in a bottle from Dr. Dorster!"

"I think you are right, Son. I had felt badly that the only real value of the original message for loved ones of Dr. Dorster, was the confirmation of his death. But this speech opens up a whole new door of possibilities. Isn't it wonderful that Clara and Thom were able to get this to me before my appointment tomorrow?"

"This whole development is nothing short of amazing," affirmed Richard.

Harold called to his passengers, "Gloria and Richard – we are within sight of our first stop. Would you like to get a view from up here?"
"Yes, that would be great!" answered Gloria. Richard came with her into the cockpit.

"This is Ponta Delgado coming into view. It is the largest of the Azore Islands. We will be here long enough to refill our fuel tanks and we can get a very nice lunch at the restaurant in the Airport. The Azores are known for their chicken recipes and also their stew beef. I guarantee that you have never tasted anything like this! Now, you have just enough time to get into your seats and seat belts, prepared for landing."

"Thank you, Sir. That view was worth seeing," said Richard.

Gloria and Richard buckled their belts, held each other's hand, and closed their eyes. This would be their first landing ever! When they felt the first bounce of the wheels and the screech of the brakes they held their breath. When the rolling stopped, they smiled at each other. Their smile said, "We are still alive! Thank God!"

Harold opened the cabin door and let down the folding stair case. He went out first so that he could extend a helping hand to Gloria. Richard and the three crewmen followed.

Richard and Gloria noticed that a fuel truck was already approaching the plane. It was good to be on the ground again, if only for a few minutes.

The restaurant was nicely furnished but "homey". It did not give the impression that it had been unduly influenced by tourism. The waitress spoke beautiful English and helped them with their understanding of the menu.

There was only one word that adequately described the

food – fabulous! "This is going to make my sandwiches taste pretty sad tonight, Boys!" complained Gloria.

"Don't say that, Mom. Your sandwiches are always delicious."

"Thanks, Richard. I really wasn't asking for that, but it is very welcome! Gentlemen. I must say that your choice of restaurants was first rate. That pretty waitress knew all of your names, too. I am impressed!"

The crew smiled. Harold said, "We have been coming here for several weeks now. We are never here for very long, though. Now, Bermuda is a different story. We always have a day there to see the sights. Oh, and this might be a good time to explain something. Our flight from London to Kingston is in three legs of just over 7 hours each. We are allowed to fly two 7 hour legs with two pilots, if we stagger our flying time – neither pilot actually flying the plane more than 8 hours during that 14 hour period. So, the way we handle it is this: Our present crew flies the 14 plus hours from London to Bermuda. Another crew, which is temporarily stationed in Bermuda, will meet us there and take the plane on the last 7 hour leg through Nassau to Kingston, Jamaica. That crew will rest a day and then bring the plane back to Bermuda. Then our crew will fly from Bermuda to London."

"In that way, no one gets overly tired and everything is much safer. So, tonight at about 9:00, we will refuel in

Bermuda. If you two are asleep, we won't bother you. If you are awake, you might want to go in and get some tea or coffee. That way you can meet the other crew before we leave.

"You know, I was wondering how you two guys could stay awake for that whole 22 hour flight. That's good to know," said Richard.

"We will miss you though. You all have been great hosts," chimed Gloria.

"Thank you, Ma'am, chorused the crew.

Richard and Gloria each brought a favorite book to read on the flight. As they settled down to read, Richard said, "Mom, have you given any thought to the possibility of staying the extra week as a matter of choice? After all, it will not cost the military any more for us to stay. It will cost us more but we were prepared to pay the whole cost of the trip if it had been necessary. We will probably never have another chance for a vacation like this in our whole life time."

"No, actually I had not thought that far ahead, Richard. But you certainly have a good point. We could afford to do that without being too hard on our savings! Let's keep an open mind about that possibility!"

"Let's!" repeated Richard, with a definite sparkle in his eye.

After an afternoon of reading, Gloria looked at her watch. It was 6:00. She walked into the cockpit. "Is anybody getting hungry in here?"

Harold said, "Knowing these guys, the answer is definitely 'yes!' Would you like for me to get the vittles? I had them in a little cooler in the galley."

"Yes, thank you Harold."

"Let me show you where the galley is and I'll get some little serving trays also."

Gloria found a little water faucet and glasses and some ice. She fixed six glasses of water and set them at each persons station, keeping two for her and Richard. Then she presented each with a paper plate and napkin that she had brought from home. She placed a pile of each kind of sandwich on two paper plates and let each person take one of each. Lastly she brought out the fruit – apples and bananas. There were many "Thank you's" offered, for the crew were not used to having these amenities.

Gloria quipped, "Don't let this make you guys sleepy. Richard and I are not checked out in DC4's yet!"

Harold said, "I still bet you could handle it!"

There was a general spirit of friendship in the group and everybody sensed that the present crew would soon be leaving. Harold said, "I think you will enjoy the other crew. They're not as good as we are but no one else is either!"

The other guys said, "Haw, haw, haw!"

After dinner, Richard and Gloria settled in their seats. Gloria got closer to the window and said, "Funny. I've been on here all of this time and have not looked out of the window at all. The sea is beautiful, isn't it?"

"Beautiful and lonely," mused Richard. "Think of those guys in that little rubber dinghy – 22 days bobbing in that beautiful, lonely sea!"

Gloria added, "It makes me so grateful that we have been given a part in this drama. Just think how many pieces have fit together already and the story isn't half over yet. In fact, we have no way of knowing how far reaching that little message in a bottle might be."

"Yes, Mom. The fact is, even if it ended with your appointment with Dr. Dorster tomorrow. Even if he were to say, "OK, that's all very interesting, thanks for coming, we'll file this away as information – it would still be worth all of the effort. Even if we can make no connection with anyone who knew Bob Swithers, I would still be glad we had a part. Just what happened already with Clara makes it worth the effort!"

"I couldn't agree with you more, Honey!"

With that last observation, each of them released their seat back and relaxed, leaving their seat belts buckled.
Within minutes they were both asleep, lulled by the constant hum of the engines outside. They slept for two hours and woke up only when they heard the screech of the tires on the tarmac at the Bermuda Airport.
Gloria looked at Richard and saw that he was yawning. "I must look a wreck!"

"You look great, Mom! You always look great!"

"My dear, prejudiced son. I love you!"

"I love you too, Mom."

They stood up when the plane stopped rolling, and went into the cockpit. The crew were already standing up and stretching. Harold said, "How about some tea or coffee?"

"Sounds great," chimed the two passengers.

As they came into the coffee shop, they saw the four new crewmen sitting at a table. They had already grouped two other tables with theirs to make enough room for the six of us.

Harold said, "Gloria and Richard Parsons, I would like for you to meet the second best crew in the history of flying.

We will do away with rank from the start. Here is your pilot, Henry Grieves from London; the co pilot, Jeff Barner from Manchester; navigator, Peter Gillespie from Northampton; and co navigator, Riley Joseph from Leeds. A better group of guys you'll never meet. Fellows, meet Gloria Parsons and her son, Richard."

When everyone had responded, Henry quipped, "With that great introduction, I guess we will be paying for the coffee and tea tonight!"

The two crews briefly discussed the trip thus far and agreed that the weather offered nothing unusual . Harold said the first two legs of the flight had been picture perfect.

When they had ordered their beverages, Harold said, "With due respect to your privacy, Gloria and Richard, Commander Lawn gave me a very brief summary of why you are going to Jamaica. It would be a gift to all of us if you would share with us the message that Richard found and any details you wish to share of the results thus far. Being in the service ourselves, we will appreciate these details even more than the average citizen, I believe."

"It would give Richard and me a great deal of pleasure to do that. What are our time parameters?"

"It is hardly fair to ask you to do it in just twenty minutes, but that is the time that we have left."

"It is enough," said Gloria. "I do have the message in my purse. I will ask my son to give the background and details of his finding the message and then read the message itself."

She then gave a summary of the experience with Clara and then read the speech that Jim had reported from Dr. Dorster.

The scene in the coffee shop was very similar to the first reading with Clara. In the whole group, nine sturdy men included, there was not a dry eye to be found.
Henry, the pilot of the second crew, spoke for the two crews when he said, "Mrs.Parsons and Richard, we count it a real privilege that you have shared this with us. We would consider it another gift if you would let us have a bit of a final report when all of the results are in. We know, of course, that we will never know all of the far reaching results of this message."

"Thank you, Henry. We will certainly keep you informed through, eh..Commander Lawn.

And please let me be Gloria and not Mrs. Parsons."

"Agreed by all, Gloria!" replied Henry.

Everyone returned to their places. The first crew retired to a vehicle that had been provided for their use. The new crew ushered their passengers into the plane and secured the cabin door.

The crew took their positions and after a few minutes of reviewing their check list, they headed down the runway for the last leg of their voyage.

Buckled in their seats, Gloria and Richard had their own private thoughts.

Gloria realized that she had never heard of Thom's retired rank, "Commander Lawn", That is impressive!"

Richard thought to himself, "I wonder how Clara is doing these last several days. I hope things are looking up in her life!"

Chapter 12. "A Spark".

Our last chapter ended with Richard thinking to himself, "I wonder how Clara is doing these last several days. I hope things are looking up in her life!" Let us let Gloria and Richard continue their flight to Jamaica while we look in on Clara and see for ourselves if "things are looking up in her life". Is it possible that a spark of "new life" might already be appearing?

We remember that Richard and Gloria had met Clara at Betsey Clark's house and had read Jim Stark's message to her then. She had been very shocked by this news, but the message did not come as a totally negative event. There was a great deal of relief involved in the message as well. In fact, as Clara had time to process Jim's death, she found herself in a state of gratitude that her twelve year vigil could finally come to an end. The term, "Missing In Action", can have the effect of imprisoning the person left "back home".There is no way to move forward. There is just enough hope that your loved one might be one of those few "lucky ones" who finally come home. So you wait, and wait, and wait. The message came through as a "gift of God" that finally allowed Clara to bring an end to her vigil and slowly regain some forward momentum in her life. In a way, Clara was like a butterfly breaking free out of the cocoon that had entrapped her for these twelve years. The good news was that she, as a lovely butterfly, would be ready to fly more quickly than she ever imagined.

On Sunday she came back home a day earlier than she had intended. She called her employee, Charley Gaber, and asked if he could come by the shop that afternoon. He was more than happy to come, because he had secretly been very attracted to Clara. But he had sensed from the very beginning that she had no time or emotional space for romantic or even social interests outside of the Cookie Shop enterprise. But Charley cared enough for Clara that he was willing to settle for just being near her every day.

Charley was about 35. He had grown up in London and served in the war as every able bodied boy had done. He had learned the cooking trade in the Royal Air Force and had also been a mechanic. He was working in a mechanic shop in Guildford, and not enjoying it very much, when he read an ad in the local newspaper for a cook at The Cookie Shop. He figured, "anything will beat this grease monkey job" so he applied.

As requested, he came by the shop after lunch on Sunday. When he saw that Clara was not in the shop, he went on up the stairs and knocked on her door. She opened the door and invited him in. There was the smell of tea and some sort of cinnamon muffin in the oven. She asked if he would have tea with her and he said that he would enjoy that. She showed him to the sofa and went to fetch the food. She came back into her small living room and placed the tray on the little table in front of the sofa. She had brought a plate of the muffins and lemon for the tea – the way that Charley liked it. Then she sat down on the sofa, facing him.

Clara silently went through the ritual of serving the tea and then took a deep breath as she prepared to deliver a prepared speech to her friend.

"Charley, you and Betsey are just about the only friends I have in the whole world. I almost said 'close' friends but that would not be very accurate. I have not allowed you to be 'close', though you certainly deserved to be. I am sure that you realized that I have been less than happy, less than normal in so many ways during the whole time that you have known me. You have been very understanding about that, I suppose, because you knew all about Jim Stark, that we had planned to be married, and that he had become missing in action twelve years ago."

"With that said, something happened last night that has changed all of that. I asked you to come by this afternoon for two reasons. First, I needed to be able to tell this to someone because the very telling of it will help me, I believe, in the processing of what has happened. Secondly, you, as one of my friends, deserve to hear what I am going to tell you. The other friend, Betsey, already knows."

Charley sat quietly. He had no way of knowing whether what he was about to hear was going to be very good news or very bad. But he sensed that it was very important to

Clara and, as such, would effect his life in some very big way in the immediate future. He braced himself for whatever was coming.

Clara told him about the visit of the mother and son that he had met earlier in the shop. She gave the background of how Richard had found a bottle in the ocean and she read her copy of the message. She said, "Charley, this has been a devastating thing to hear, because I loved Jim dearly. But in a way it is one of those experiences like seeing some one that you love waste away with cancer. You love them but you reach a point when you are relieved that their suffering is over even if it is death that takes the suffering away. So, knowing finally that Jim is dead has made me sad but it has also given me the chance to face life with hope and joy again."

"I wanted you to know about this because I will need you to be patient with me as I work through this. I am probably going to have times when I am sad and crying and some other times when I am moody, maybe even angry for no apparent reason. But you have seen all of that before. The good news is that maybe I can see some light at the 'end of the tunnel' now. I have to say that I was never able to see that light before!"

"Clara, I....."

"Just one more thing, Charley, before you say anything. If I don't say it now I might lose my courage. I have sensed that you have some feelings for me that you have not voiced out of respect for my situation. If I am wrong about that, then I apologize and I am embarrassed that I have misinterpreted . You might be surprised for me to say that I have had feelings for you that I have not allowed myself to even admit before today. I know that I am not being very 'lady like' and I am blushing with embarrassment. You must think that I am awful..."

"Now, Clara, you must allow me to speak now while I have my courage up too. You are NOT awful. Words can not express how 'un–awful' I think you are. I know that what you just told me took all the courage in the world for you to express so much of yourself to me when you were not really sure how I would take it or how I felt. I don't have the best words in the world when it comes to telling what is in my heart. But I am going to try. Clara, if there is a chance in the world that I can have a place in your future, then I am willing to wait as long as it takes. My feelings for you are much deeper than I have the right to tell you yet. Right now, if......well, I've said enough. I don't want to scare you off."

"Charley, there is no way in this world that you could scare me off ! I'm sure of that!"
"Then, would you mind very much if I gave you a hug?"
"I would mind very much if you didn't!"
Clara and Charley hugged for a very long moment and much was said without a word as the deep feelings in each were translated in silent energy.

Finally, Charley said, "Now, Clara, I hope that our being so frank today is not going to "mess up" our working together from now on."

"Not at all, Charley. Tomorrow morning I'll still be the 'boss lady' and you'll still be the employee. That is, unless you've been saving your money to buy into the Cookie Shop. In that case we would be 'Partners'!"

"I am working towards that too, Clara."

"Being the boss lady won't keep me from getting an occasional hug, I hope. I kind of enjoyed that!"
"Anything you say, boss lady! See you tomorrow!"

Clara watched Charley walk down the stairs. "Would you check on that batch of fudge cookies in the cooler, Charlie? I don't want them too hard."

"Sure will, Clara. Thanks for the tea. Those cinnamon muffins were top notch!"

As Charley closed the front door of the shop, Clara found herself smiling for the first time in a very long time. Clara thought to herself, "What was it that Charley said? 'Right now, if.....' I wonder what he was about to say?"

Chapter 13. "The Arrival".

Gloria and Richard have slept through most of their seven and a half hour trip from Bermuda. The plane was refueled in Nassau, but the passengers slept through that brief stop. At about 3:00 A.M., Gloria awoke and went into the cockpit. "Good morning, all!"

"Good morning", echoed the crew.

"Henry, I have a question that we certainly should have asked before, and I am embarrassed to ask it now. But this is the first time that it has occurred to me."

"What is that, dear Lady?"

"Well, I thought of Jamaica as being very small, with most everything of importance being either in or near Kingston. I felt sure that a school of higher learning would be somewhere close to Kingston."

"Ok, and your question is...?"

"Do you know how far Mandeville is from Kingston?"

"Sure! We have been all over Jamaica. Mandeville is about 2 to 2 1/2 hours drive from the Airport in Kingston. Is Mandeville where you are headed?"

"Yes Sir. I had figured it would be a short taxi drive at most! Oh my! What have I done? I have scheduled an appointment with a professor in a school in Mandeville at 9:00 this morning!"

"I don't really see any problem with that unless it is what you will do to fill up your extra time. We should get into Kingston at 4:00. That is 5 hours to make a 2 ½ hour trip."

"But do you think a bus will be running between those two cities at that time of the morning? Or will there be a taxi that will be available so early?"

"Oh, Gloria, now I see what you are worried about. Oh, No,No,No. You are not going to hire transportation! I thought you realized....well, no, obviously no one thought to tell you. Well, here is the system. Each crew is assigned a vehicle in their anchor city. The other crew has a car in Bermuda. We have one in Kingston. We have always intended to take you to wherever you needed to go. We will also pick you up when you are ready to come back, whether it is tomorrow or next Friday! I guess we just assumed that the other crew had told you."

"Oh, Henry. You can not imagine how much worry you just took off of me! Thank you so much! But how can you do that after having just flown for seven and a half hours?"

"Well, first of all, the whole crew doesn't do the drive, just one of the crew that had not piloted or navigated during the last segment from Nassau. So, whoever is driving the car has rested for several hours before touch down in Kingston. Secondly, soon after we started allowing passengers – and passengers are always on important business, not just sight seeing – we discovered that many of the destinations were other than Kingston. So most folks had the same problem as you did – how to get across the island at 4:00 in the morning? So, we solved the problem by just taking everyone where they needed to go. In your case, we will get to Mandeville at about 7:00, which gives us time to get a good breakfast at a great restaurant and then allow you two time to freshen up before your appointment. Then I will do my reports while you have your appointment. Everything fits together beautifully. I will be your driver because Jeff has been flying the last leg from Nassau."

"Well, I must say, the Navy has really worked this all out perfectly!"

"The Navy AND the Royal Air Force! Remember, it is a joint venture!"

Gloria went back to her seat and saw that Richard was still sleeping soundly. She was totally awake and beyond getting back to sleep. Besides, there was only about 30 minutes before touch down in Kingston. She began to imagine what her appointment would be like. She rehearsed what she would say in the beginning. After all, the only thing that Dr. Leitman Dorster had been told was that Gloria "had information about his brother." They had been careful not to mention his death prematurely.

Gloria remembered to buckle her seat belt as she felt the now familiar landing pattern form – a slight bank and a ninety degree turn followed by a slight slowing sound of the motors. She touched Richard gently to wake him for the descent and touch down. Richard smiled a groggy grin and they held hands as the angle of descent increased. Gloria was surprised that neither of them closed their eyes this time. They were becoming "seasoned fliers".

When the rolling stopped, Gloria and Richard stood up, stretched, and yawned. As they walked into the cockpit, there were "good mornings' all around. Jeff said, "Henry will help you folks out while I retrieve your bags from the luggage compartment."

"Thank you, Jeff! Thank all four of you fellows for giving us a safe and enjoyable trip. We will look forward to seeing you on the return."
"Will you be with us tomorrow, Gloria?" asked Peter.

"I don't really know yet, Peter. There is a good chance that we will stay until next Friday."

Richard beamed a smile quietly.
The plane had rolled to a lighted area and one lone attendant was driving a small vehicle out to do some sort

of service or security procedure. The two navigators grabbed the suit cases as Henry led the way to the car. "We will be a little tight in the car for a few minutes until we get these three to our quarters", said Henry. "It is only about three miles down the road".

"An English Ford," said Gloria. "I know someone that has one just like this, only it's blue instead of gray."

"Might you be speaking of Commander Lawn, by any chance?" asked Jeff.

"Yes, actually, I am! How did you know?"

"Just a guess. He's the only one I know with a blue one".

"He must be quite well known." queried Gloria.

"Quite well. He is very well thought of by the Navy men in the London area. He is the 'Navy's friend in government' you might say. I don't mean that he gives us any unfair advantage. But he does tend to protect us from those who might want to save money by cutting us out of the budget in drastic ways."

It was a bit like a circus clown act to see six adults fit themselves carefully into a car that was designed for four passengers. They all laughed as the little English Ford purred down the road for its three mile exertion.

They let the three crewmen out at their quarters and Henry began the two hour plus trip to Mandeville. The roads were fairly decent by European standards – two lanes most of the way.

Henry, being from London, knew the neighborhood where Gloria had grown up. She mentioned that she had a teacher by the name of Grieves at Griggs Elementary School. "That was my Aunt Emma!" Henry answered. "Small world! I hope she wasn't too mean."

"On the contrary, she was very nice, and a very good teacher as I remember", affirmed Gloria.

Richard spent his time looking at all of the sights along the way. Everything was so different from what he was used to in England. He was just constantly amazed.

Just before 7:00, Henry pulled up to a very nice looking restaurant on Perth Road in Mandeville. But the lights were not on in front. Gloria read, " 'Bloomfield Greathouse Restaurant'. It's a nice looking place but it isn't open, Henry."

"Right," said Henry. "It is only open for lunch and dinner. But we are going to have a private dining experience. You see, the cook and the owner meet for breakfast every morning to plan the day. They enjoy the fellowship, and they have really spoiled us Service personnel. I can absolutely guarantee you a wonderful welcome!"

"OK, if you say so, Henry."

Gloria and Richard reluctantly followed Henry around to the back door and Henry knocked. The door opened and a big Italian fellow opened the door and literally yelled.

"Pilot Officer Henry Grieves! Oh, itsa you! Come in, Come in – and your friends, Come into my kitchen!"

"Gloria and Richard, I want you to meet Luigi Paterno – the best cook in all of Jamaica! With him is Lou Armitage, the marvelous owner of Bloomfield! Luigi and Lou, please meet my good friends, Gloria Parsons and her son, Richard."

"We are just having breakfast, my friends, and we will be honored for you to please join us!" said Luigi with his strong Italian accent. "How do you prefer your eggs? Please call it out and I will do it!"

"Scrambled, please," answered Henry.

"I would like that too," followed Gloria.

"I would like mine fried over light, please." added Richard.

They all sat down and enjoyed a jovial feast of eggs, sausage, bacon, tropical fruit, sweet breads of several varieties, and coffee, tea, or milk.

They enjoyed themselves until 8:15 and Henry told Lou, "We are expected at the West Indian Training School at 9:00. Can you tell us how long that will take? It is on Manchester Road."

"Ten minutes at the most, Pilot Officer Grieves. It is just up the road and there won't be much traffic."

"Would you mind if Mrs. Parsons and Richard use your restroom facilities to freshen up? They have been on the plane since 6:00 A.M. yesterday?"

"Oh I will be delighted for them to make themselves feel at home. I will show them where it is."

After a very happy farewell, the three travelers got into the English Ford. "I have never been so content," said Richard.
"I will be very lucky if I do not go to sleep while making our presentation to Dr. Dorster! said Gloria.

In just ten minutes they were pulling up to the front door of the West Indian Training School. It was a building that obviously had been "added to" on countless occasions. The main building was a two story brick building, but there were smaller wooden buildings on each side of the main building. Gloria and Richard would later observe that there were four similar wooden structures in the area behind the brick building.

Henry said, "Gloria, I will go in with you and ask for a separate area where I can write out my reports of the flight. I want you to take as long as you need to. Please do not feel rushed. I have absolutely no other duty but to be at your service for the rest of the day."

"Thank you so much, Henry. I really appreciate that!"
"Henry parked the car and they all three entered the front door of the main building.

The secretary looked up from her desk. "Mrs. Parsons and Richard?"
"Yes, I am Gloria Parsons, this is my son, Richard, and this is Pilot Officer Henry Grieves who has been so kind as to bring us all the way from Kingston this morning."

"Oh, we are so very glad that you have come! Dr. Dorster and his sister, Cassia, are waiting for you in his office. I will show you to Dr. Dorster's office."

"Pilot Officer Grieves will not be going in with us but he would like to have a place where he can complete his written report of the flight, if that can be arranged."added Gloria.

"Oh, yes Mum. I will be glad to take care of that."

"Now, if you will follow me, they are very anxious to meet you."

Gloria tried to quiet the anxiety that had built up during the last 24 hours concerning this meeting. "Would they be well received? What would Dr. Leitman Dorster be like? Would there be a problem in communication?" Well, she was about to find out - ready or not!

Chapter 14. "The Appointment".

The secretary knocked on Dr. Dorster's office door. "Come in, please" spoke a very pleasant but masculine voice.

The secretary announced, in a butler like, formal fashion: "Dr. Dorster and Miss Dorster, may I present Mrs. Gloria Parsons and her son, Richard. Mrs. Parsons and Mr. Parsons, please meet Dr. Leitman Dorster and his sister, Miss Cassia Dorster."

Everyone said the proper words and the secretary left and closed the door. Dr. Dorster quickly got up and held the chair for Gloria. He showed Richard to the chair next to her. All four were sitting in a comfortable semicircle. The room was cozy – more like a home library than an office.

Dr. Dorster spoke first. "Mrs. Parsons and Richard. I certainly want to thank you both, first of all, for coming such a long distance on our behalf. As you can imagine, we have been very anxiously awaiting your arrival and for the information that you have concerning our brother. To be quite honest, we have not allowed ourselves to be optimistic in our expectations. After this long period, we expect that this news must be sad. But in this case I would rephrase the old adage 'no news is good news' to say 'sad news is better than no news'. We have certainly found that 'no news' is a very difficult thing to deal with."

Gloria sat in her chair, feeling inside like a teen aged girl who sees her first "Rock Star" in person. She is almost overwhelmed by the sight of these two individuals. He is the personification of Errol Flynn and Gregory Peck, dressed impeccably and speaking the "King's English" better than the King! His sister, though she has not spoken yet, looks like she just walked out of Buckingham Palace ready to receive Royalty.

The gravity of the occasion fell upon Gloria, finally, and lesser thoughts were pushed aside. She took a deep breath and cleared her throat. "Dr. Dorster and Miss Dorster. I am very sorry to say that you are correct in expecting my information to be sad. We have good reason to believe that your brother did not survive the war. We have come this far because we wanted to present, personally, what we have. I have asked Richard to relate the story to you just as it happened to him."

"Yes. May I say, 'thank you, Dr. Dorster and Miss Dorster for allowing us to come!' To begin with, we have a friend who has a cottage at Brighton Beach, near London, which has a long sea front beach. They allow us to use the cottage on occasions. This was my seventeenth birthday and my mother and I were there for the week end. I had ridden my bike down to the boat dock and had fished at a jetty all morning without catching anything. I was about to come in when I had a sudden urge to go out by one of the marker buoys. I could not shake that urge so I decided to row on over. When I got there I immediately saw a small bottle bobbing in the water, surrounded by a brown foam. I picked up the bottle and found, to my surprise, that there seemed to be a piece of paper inside. I was very excited, of course, and rowed back as quickly as I could. I placed the bottle in my back pack and raced to the cottage on my bike."

"I took the bottle to the kitchen, called my Mom, placed the bottle on the table, and turned on the over head light. I told my Mother what I had and she brought a magnifying glass in case their was a message that was hard to read. I pulled out the cork and fished out the rolled up paper with long tweezers. I unrolled the brittle paper carefully onto the table and to our surprise we found the following message:

"I write these words to no one special. I have no family, except for one. But somehow it makes dying easier if you say some sort of last words. I don't expect anybody to find this so I write it as a statement to the 'cloud of witnesses' that the Bible says is watching me. I am floating in a little rubber life raft. The supplies aboard have long ago been used up, except for this bit of paper and pencil and a bottle that I saved. My ship went down from a German sub. Most of my buddies went down with the ship.

Three of us found this dinghy. The other two Bob Swithers and Melvin Dorster have already died from exposure and, I think, loss of hope. We have counted twenty days. I am

Jim Stark of London. I am very weak and feel that my time can be a matter of minutes or hours at the most.
I want to say that I hope that what we are trying to do to turn Hitler around will work. I hope that peace will some day come back to the England that I love. But I want the world to know that, no matter who wins this war, I, Jim Stark, believe that freedom will win over tyranny wherever the two may meet. Freedom has within its own seed the fruit of triumph. Tyranny likewise has within its own seed the fruit of failure. God and the nature of life will see to that.

And so I die with full confidence that my dying alone on this drifting sea is not in vain and I will watch the inevitable victory march of human freedom from some grand stand seat among my buddies, somewhere up there. Know that I die in full hope of living again. Love to all, Jim Stark, March, 1942."

There was a long silence to give Dr. and Miss Dorster time to absorb the words that they had just heard. Then Gloria said, "I know how difficult it must be for you to hear this beautiful message and to know that it says so little about your brother, other than that he had died. But that is not the end of the information that we have. We had already shared this message with Clara Woolsey of London, who was supposed to marry the Jim Stark of the message when he returned from that voyage. We were as sad for her as we are for you."

"While we were on the plane coming to Jamaica, however, Clara began reviewing her letters from Jim. She came across information in one of her letters that she knew would help you. So she got in touch with Sir Thomas Lawn, who has been very helpful to us in this whole enterprise, and she shared her finding with him. He also knew that it would be of value to you, so he sent the whole message by radio to the plane and I have it here for you. I believe that what we are going to share with you will lift your spirits considerably. That is certainly our hope! I will read the information exactly as Clara read it in her letter: "Clara, do you remember that I mentioned a sailor that is actually a college professor, in civilian life? His name is Dr. Melvin Dorster. Well, they got him in the Navy mainly because he is going to represent Jamaica when we christen the new cruiser, HMS Jamaica in May of this year. He is to be the Dedicatory Speaker. His bunk is right under mine and last night he was quietly rehearsing his speech but I was able to hear every word. Something he said really stuck in my mind and I wanted to pass it on to you before I forget it because to me it is really special.
Listen to this. It is almost word for word as he said it."

" 'It has been a profound gift to me, as a citizen of Jamaica, to have had the privilege of knowing the young men who are serving so bravely in this war. I think of their courage and their sincere devotion to country, to God, and to truth. But this war will not last forever. And these young men and those young women who are showing their courage back home even now – they will need to find schools that are worthy of nourishing their good minds, schools that will receive them with open arms.' "

" 'I, for one, have been given a new vision of the need for those schools to have the very highest of standards and goals. As a person who has some influence in such a school, I plan to go back to the country for which this fine ship is named, and help to establish one of the finest Universities in the Western Hemisphere. With God's help and the help of my fellow countrymen, it WILL happen!' "

Gloria finished by saying, "This is my copy. I have not had a chance to get it reproduced yet. But you are welcome to it, Dr. Dorster."

"We can copy it right here in the office, Mrs. Parsons," said Dr. Dorster. Give us just a moment to 'catch our breath' after that. There was a long pause as Dr. Dorster looked at his sister and patted her hand. Then he said, Mrs. Parsons and Richard, I can not tell you in words what a difference this last information makes to us, but I will try."

"It goes far beyond what any of us in this room can possibly imagine. You see, the West Indies Training School was begun as an attempt by the Seventh Day Adventist Church to make a difference in the lives of the young people here in Jamaica. It was begun in 1907 and finally worked its way up to having students from the first through the twelfth grades. It struggled for many years, but with the vision of several professors, including Melvin, and by the way, could we just use first names among friends here?"

"That will be fine with us, Leitman."

"Leit is what my friends call me. So, as I was saying, we struggled for many years and finally we were able to add Theology, Teaching, Secretarial Science, and Natural Science to our curriculum. But you see, when we lost Melvin, we lost much of our spirit and momentum. Melvin had such energy and vision! When we lost him, our Faculty and our Board of Directors just seemed to lose their heart and their enthusiasm for improving our school. I have often thought that, if only Melvin had not been lost we would have had our full university here in Jamaica now! But you see, this speech that you have brought – it sounds just LIKE him! It has enough emotional energy in its words to restart a flame of hope for 'one of the finest universities in the Western Hemisphere!' "

"Yes, said Gloria. "Richard and I had sensed that ourselves."

"Now, Gloria, you and Richard must present this to several groups, just as you have done it this morning. There is the Faculty and the Board of Directors. Then there is the Education Committee of our government in Kingston that will definitely want you to speak to them. No doubt this will lead to interest in several other civic groups both here in Mandeville and also in Kingston. I can easily arrange for all of this! I do hope that you are prepared to stay for several days!"

Gloria looked at Richard, who was beaming and moving his head affirmatively – trying hard to appear more mature than his seventeen year old enthusiasm would permit.

"Yes, Leit. We have the alternative of going back tomorrow or staying until next Friday morning. So, yes, we would be honored to stay if you wish."

"May I say a word, Gloria?"
"Of course, Cassia!"

"I haven't spoken before now, but I would like to affirm all that Leit has said about the importance of these two messages for our family but especially for our school and for the young and old people of Jamaica itself. They NEED a University. But you both are an important factor in this being presented in the powerful way that is needed here. We can not recreate for Jamaica what you have done for us this morning unless you are involved!"

"So, as the woman of the Dorster household, let me offer our home to be your home, our vehicle to be at your disposal, and (smiling) Gloria, I believe my size 10 wardrobe will fit you very nicely!"

Gloria looked at Richard with a look that said, "What do you think, Son?"

Richard said, "Yes! Yes!"

Gloria said, "Leit and Cassia, we humbly accept your generous offer of hospitality and we pledge to do anything we can to help in the effort to bring about Melvin's dream!"

"Wonderful, said Leit. Then your first assignment will be to join Cassia and Me on our sailboat this afternoon. There will be a number of Faculty and Students aboard and they will be eager to meet you both. Cassia has a size 10 swim suit for you, Gloria, and I am sure that one of my suits will fit Richard."

"But first we must fetch Rachel, our Secretary, and your young Naval Officer. It is almost time for lunch, and there is an exquisite restaurant not far from here. It is called the Bloomfield Greathouse Restaurant."

Chapter 15. "A Day On the Ocean".

Leit and Cassia led the way and found that Rachel and Henry had already become well acquainted. Leit explained in a good natured way that they had decided not to release Gloria and Richard to the Navy for another week, but that they would have them back at the Airport in Kingston by 5:30 A.M. On Friday. He also said that he would not take "no" for and answer to an invitation to lunch. Henry agreed and said that he would go in his own vehicle since the restaurant was on the way to Kingston. He also asked if Leit would trust him with his secretary if he promised to be careful. Leit said, "I think I can trust a man who just brought Gloria safely all the way from Bermuda. But of course, Rachel will have to have the last word on that. But, I would wager that the last word will be 'yes'."

So, Henry and Rachel got in the English Ford and Leit, Cassia, Gloria, and Richard were in the school's vehicle, which was a 1952 Nash Ambassador!

On the way Gloria said, "Leit, I have a confession to make and I do not want to take away from your wonderful idea of going to Bloomfield. We did have breakfast there this morning and we are definitely looking forward to lunch. I would not have mentioned it except I knew that the wonderful cook, Luigi, and the generous owner, Lou, would give it away as soon as they saw me."

Sure enough, as soon as they entered the front door of the restaurant, Lou said, "There is my good friends Leit, Cassia, and Henry and they have brought our new friends, Gloria and Richard. And I see that Henry has 'discovered' Rachel! Ah! Wait until I tell Luigi. He will be happy!"

Lou directed them to "the best table". I will send Luigi to tell you what is the very best lunch for today!"

Luigi came out and gave them a brief description of the best fish recipe, the best chicken dish, and the best beef in the house. Everyone went with the fish.

As they had fellowship around the table, Gloria realized that there were some important details that no one knew except she and Richard. So she told about all that had happened with Betsey and Clara and then about all of the helpful contributions that Sir Thomas had made.

Then Leit and Cassia alternated in telling the group about the development of the school and of their own upbringing with Melvin.

By the time lunch and the good fellowship was finished, it was 1:30. Leit invited Henry to go on the sail boat cruise with them. But Henry declined in favor of getting back to his quarters for some sleep for tomorrow's flight. Henry asked, "Are you going on the boat, Rachel?"

Rachel said, "No. I really need to be at the school. This time of year we do get inquiries about enrollment, etc. So I really need to be there with the telephone."

"Well, I do have time to take you back to the school if you don't mind."

"I would like that very much, Henry!" she replied (to no one's surprise!).

"We have about two hours to get to the boat," said Leit. "We said we would shove off at 3:30. We can go by our house and get our swim suits and towels and then go by the school for the bus. We are expecting twenty five on the boat, including us four. The students will go on the bus and there will probably be about three faculty on the bus and about five others coming in cars. The boat is anchored at Long Bay, which is about a thirty minute drive from home."

Gloria had begun to feel very comfortable with Leit and Cassia and the same seemed to be the case with Richard. They had a way of making a person feel as though they had known him a long time. As they traveled to Leit's and Cassia's home, they alternated in labeling the homes they passed - "This is where Arthur Harrington lives. He is in the Theology school. Here is Owen Goddard's house. He teaches in the Business School. You will meet him and Polly on the boat. Here is our Community Play House. They usually have a music group on Friday nights. We would like to take you there tomorrow night if you don't mind."

"That sounds good!" said, Gloria.

"I hope you will not feel abused," said Leit., "But we will have you such a short time we feel as though we should 'fish in every pond', so to speak. So, what we will probably do is ask permission for you and Richard to speak briefly concerning your experience with the message and then I would apply what you have said to a proposal that I would like to make concerning the 'Melvin Dorster Foundation for a new University'. We should be able to do the whole thing in twenty minutes without reducing the impact of the message. Do you think we could do that? I know that the people will be thrilled to hear what you will share. There should be at least 300 people there and they will be a good cross section of our community."

"That makes sense to me," affirmed Gloria.

"May I ask what kind of music?" requested Richard.

"We have a good variety. Sometimes it is a Chamber Music group from Kingston. Tomorrow night I believe it is a popular 'Mento' band, called 'Wiggins!. Of course, 'Mento' is our word for what some call Jamaican Calypso. I think you will both like it."

"I have several Mento recordings and enjoy that style for its wide variety – sometimes strictly fun and sometimes very serious," said Richard.

When they arrived at the Dorster home, Leit and Cassia excused themselves for a moment and then brought out a swim suit and jacket for Gloria and Richard. "The jacket might feel good when the breeze gets up on the ship," said Cassia. "Now this will be your room. I hope twin beds will be O.K."

"They look very comfortable," said Gloria.
"We'll leave you to change. Just come on out when you are ready!"

They went to the school, which was only about a mile away. Leit and Cassia introduced Richard and Gloria to each of the students and faculty as they came on the bus. Then the four of them took adjoining seats so they could talk on the way to Long Bay, where the boat was docked. The route was interesting. There were nice homes on the edge of town and then for miles there were mostly little huts with what looked like straw roofs here and there, sitting back from the highway. The conversation was mostly about Gloria, her marriage and loss of Richard, Sr., and Richard's experience thus far in school.

Without warning, the highway began an abrupt descent and in the distance one could see the vast expanse of the Caribbean Sea. Almost immediately they were at the boat. Everyone disembarked and joined the others who had come in cars. They walked up on the dock and then over a bridge like walk way onto the boat.

Leit was, indeed, the captain. He had trained two students to assist him on the boat and they untied the ropes joining to the dock. Leit started the auxiliary engine to take them out to deeper water and when they had cleared the shallows and found open water the sails were unfurled.

"Oh, my Heavens!" yelled Gloria. She had never seen or heard such an exciting few minutes in her whole life. It absolutely took her breath away. "Oh, I can't believe that! Why, I'd like to see that again! It was over too quickly! Oh, I am a sailor at heart and never knew it! I've always liked boats and the sea but I've never....Oh!"

Leit and Cassia were laughing. "We are not laughing AT you, Gloria. We are laughing from the shear joy of seeing someone else experience the unfurling for the very first time. It is one of the exquisite delights of living in Jamaica!"

The boat itself was a 55 ft., three mast Schooner with a beam (width) of 10 ft. It had been a fishing vessel until 1949 when the owners went to a more high tech ship and sold the Schooner at a very good price to the Dorsters. Since the purpose of the boat was, to a great extent, for the use of students and faculty, the school sponsored the renovation. They redid the interior to be primarily a large room with built in seating for approximately 25 passengers in an "in the round" configuration.

There was also a galley, a restroom, and four small cots, allowing two couples to go on an overnight trip. Besides the auxiliary engine to move the boat, there was a small gasoline generator to provide lighting and electricity for a two way radio and their record player. Most of the activities in good weather would be carried out on the deck. There was also a small launch boat that carried six passengers at a time for ship to shore transfer.

The students and faculty, about 20 plus the four of them, were in high spirits. They congregated in several open spaces near the ships wheel. One of the students brought a guitar and a teacher had a banjo. They sang popular songs, folk songs, Jamaican Mento songs, and religious hymns and choruses. Gloria and Richard knew the words of most of the songs until they got to the strictly Jamaican songs. They did know "Drinking Rum and Coca Cola", which enjoyed popularity all over the world. Of course, some of the faculty frowned a bit on that one.

Gloria went over and stood by Leit. "I want to thank you for this! It would have been such a loss for Richard and me if we had missed this. It has literally been years since I have felt this open and free"

Leit said, "That is Jamaica, Gloria! When Melvin and I went to the U.S. To the University of Florida for undergraduate work and then for our Doctorate, we missed Jamaica terribly. We did not have an abundance of funds because we knew that Cassia would be making the same trek in three more years. So we only came home once or twice a year. I almost quit once before I finished my doctorate – simply because I missed this! - So much! To me, this is the next thing to Heaven itself.!"

"Now, when this song is over, I am going to make an announcement and then in a few minutes I will introduce you and Richard. Then I will say a few words to tie what you have said to our school situation. We can sort of let it be a rehearsal for tomorrow night. O.K.?"

"That sounds fine to me, Leit."
When the song was over, Leit said, "Folks, I hope everyone is having a good time. We have two very special guests with us this afternoon. I think all of you have met Gloria and Richard. But you do not know why they are here. You have all heard about Dr. Melvin Dorster, my brother. You also know that he disappeared twelve years ago, while serving in the Royal Navy. Well, Gloria and Richard have some information about Dr. Dorster. It is sad news, but it is also uplifting news. So I will ask you to sing two more songs and then they will share their message with us. Please sing 'White Cliffs of Dover' and 'We Are Never Far Away'. Then we will listen to our new friends."

They sang the first song, which reminded them of the war years. And then they sang this:

"We are never far from each other, Even when we can not

see a face.
We are never far from our brother, Even when he's in
another place.

Even when we can't hear his voice, And though his
absence be without his choice,

If by faith we know he's with the Father, Then we know
we're never far away."

When the group ended their song, Richard stood up and
told his part of the story. He continued to stand as Gloria
stood and continued her part. Then they both continued to
stand as Leit let one of the working students replace him at
the wheel and then came and told them what he felt was
his brother's dream – to build a new University for
Jamaica.

As he finished he said, "Let us all hold hands in a circle.
Then he began to sing,

"Dear Alma Mater share with us your knowledge,

Trusting we look to thee as our source of learning.

We would prepare ourselves for the life abundant,

Teach us the way of Truth!"

Gloria was impressed by the beauty of their school song

and the heartfelt way in which they sang. After the singing of the Alma Mater, Leit said that all three of them were open for any questions that the group might have. There were questions for at least ten minutes concerning details of the bottle and the message, the flight to Jamaica, and questions concerning Gloria and Richard's own lives in London.

Then Leit announced, "You are free to do as you wish for the next 45 minutes while some of the ladies rustle up some vittles from the galley. Thank you for your good attention. Stay on deck until you hear the dinner bell ring. Thanks."

Cassia lead the faculty wives to the galley where bread, meat, cheese, etc. waited for sandwich making.. There would also be beverages, chips, and cookies on paper plates.

Gloria was glad to see that Richard had been "absorbed" by several new friends – one of which was a very pretty young lady.

She walked back to the ship's wheel where Leit had again taken control. "Leit, it is amazing to me how beautifully this ship flies through the waves. It is a marvelous feeling - so much more than simply being in a pram or canoe!"

"Yes, it helps explain why men like Jim Stark and my brother loved the Navy so much. We did get several letters from Melvin and, even though he was just in the Navy for a specific purpose, he had really fallen in love with sailing. He had never done any sailing before going to England. Your husband had been in the Navy if I remember correctly. Did he like the Navy?"

"Oh yes. I have no doubt that he would have stayed if he had not been hurt."

"Do you have any other family in England?"

"Just a cousin or two," answered Gloria.

"So, no strong ties?"

"No strong ties! I guess I had never said or even thought that before you asked. But you know. I really don't have any strong ties in England except my job."

"Then perhaps you will get some of Jamaica's sand in your shoes. If you do you will never get rid of it, Gloria. Once it is there, you never get Jamaica's sand out of your shoes or Jamaica's spirit out of your heart!"

There was a long silence as Gloria thought of what he had said. "Am I getting Jamaica sand in my shoes?"

Chapter 16. "A 'Chemistry' Is Recognized"

Gloria had not noticed that they had been cruising back toward the dock for the last half hour. Leit wanted to be tied down before dark.

After the boat was secure, they all ate their picnic supper and headed home happily. Everyone thanked Gloria and Richard for the gift they had given.

On the way back, Gloria remembered that she was supposed to call Thom. When they got back to Mandeville she mentioned that to Leit and he set it up with the international operator. She dialed the number collect. As she waited for Thom to answer she was amazed that she had not thought of him all day. She had almost forgotten to call.

"Hello."

"Hello Thom. I am sorry I am so late but this day has been from one thing to another since I got off the plane." She gave a detailed account and indicated that there was no way at all that she could have turned down the request for her to stay. Thom understood.

"I am glad that you have that marvelous opportunity. It will do more good than any of us will ever know. Before I forget it I must tell you this. I have not found the name of Bob Swithers anywhere in Navy records. He must have been one of the ten men whose records were being transferred on the ship that went down. I will keep looking, but it doesn't look too promising. So, you might keep that in mind and keep your ears open for something that you might hear there. Perhaps Melvin wrote some passing remark about Bob to someone somewhere. It might be our only hope. OK, I would really appreciate it if you would keep me informed about how everything goes. I guess I would be selfish to ask you to call me every day. But you know, I really miss you....and Richard of course."

"I will try to call every day, Thom."

"Now, Gloria, I just want to warn you. They say 'that if you get Jamaica's sand in your shoes you can never get it out', so be careful!"

Gloria thought to herself, "Thom is trying to be cute and clever but he has no idea how true that saying is". "Yes, Thom, I have heard that same thing. I would not be surprised if there was some truth there."

Gloria pondered a strange question in the back of her mind. Even though she had thought about Thom often on the plane and had clearly missed him, she had not thought of him a single time since she met Leit. In fact, she knew Thom was inviting her to say, "I missed you too". But she could not bring herself to do it. "Strange! Jamaican sand, indeed!" she thought.

"Well, Thom, it has been a busy day and we still have to have our bath. I will try to call you earlier tomorrow if possible, but I have no idea what our schedule will be except that we plan to speak after the concert tomorrow evening. I appreciate all that you are doing. I wish that you could experience the things that we have experienced already and it is just beginning.

"I am glad to do anything I can do to help. I would love to be there with you too. It will be a very long week until you return!"

"Thank you, Thom. I'll talk with you tomorrow. Good night."

"Good night, Gloria. Please tell Richard I said good night."

"I will, Thom."

The conversation left Gloria concerned again about her feelings. She could say, "I wish that you could experience what we have experienced", but she was quite aware that she could not say, "I wish that you were here," even though she knew that he would like to have heard that. She also felt herself resenting just a little bit that she was committed to calling Thom every day. It seemed to dilute her energy and act as somewhat of a distraction right now. She wished that she could forget London altogether and just concentrate on what she was doing in Jamaica. But she certainly felt an obligation to Thom. He had done so much for her and Richard. Without Thom they would still be at "square one".

After the phone call she found Richard in their room. He was sitting quietly in a chair. "A penny for your thoughts, Richard!"

"Hi Mom. I was just reliving the boat ride. That was so great! I made a lot of friends already. Several of them have already invited me to do things."

For instance!"

"Well, there was a girl, Jacqueline, the pretty girl I was with most often, did you notice?"

"Yes."
"Well, she wants me to join her family for a fishing trip some time over the week end. She said that they are flexible as to when they can go. I am supposed to check with you and Dr. Dorster and find out when I am needed and when I am free."

"Yes, that is my question too. I suppose that we need to check with Leit and Cassia to see what their evening schedule is like. It is 8:30. Let's see if we can have a little planning session now."

"OK. We need to work in a bath time too. I feel as though I haven't had a bath in a week, and it has only been since yesterday morning."

"I'll go ask now."

Gloria went into the living room and found Leit reading the newspaper. "Hi Leit. Richard and I were wondering if we could sit down with you and Cassia some time this evening and get an idea of our schedule for the week end. He has been invited to a family fishing trip with a girl that he met on the boat – Jacqueline."

"Yes, a very sweet girl and a wonderful family. That is Jacqueline Rodriguez. I would suggest that you call her now – it isn't too late – and find out if they have a preference. We can work around most anything for Friday or Saturday, except that you need to be available to go to the concert tomorrow night at 7:00 P.M. If they want to leave very early, we can work with that also. I do have some fishing tackle if they need to use it.
"That sounds like a good approach", said Richard.

"Good. I will get her on the phone."

Leit got Jacqueline on the phone and Richard told her the alternatives that Leit had pointed out. She said, "That should be all that we need to know. Actually, we were thinking about going back to Long Bay. We have a boat there. OK. I'll call you back in a few minutes. Thanks."

The phone rang in ten minutes. Cassia answered and it was

Jacqueline for Richard.

"Hello, Richard. Do you have a pencil and paper?"

"Yes."

"OK. My folks said we would pick you up at 6:00 tomorrow morning, we will get breakfast at a little place near the Bay, be back here at noon. If you have something planned we can drop you off there. Otherwise you can come home with us while we clean the fish and we can have you back at your house by 2:00. Then, we wanted you all to come to our place to eat the fish at 5:00. That would give you plenty of time to get to the concert at 7:00. Do you have all of that?"

"Got it!"

"OK. Discuss that and let us know how that sounds."

"OK."

Richard explained the Rodriguez' plans.
Leit said, "Here's what I would like to do. I need to spend some time on the phone in the morning, setting up meetings for next week and also checking out about us speaking after the concert tomorrow night. Gloria and Cassia could have some time together then. At noon we could have a light lunch. After lunch we could run over to

a few shops in Mandeville. There are not a lot because we are not a tourist town, but there are a few nice places. Then we can see a few historical spots and be back home in time to go to the Rodriguez' home for dinner. Then, I have a couple of ideas about Saturday that we can talk about after you have talked with Jacqueline again. Right now you need to decide whether you will come back here for lunch or go with them to clean fish. If so, you can eat lunch with them. You will just miss the shopping trip. Or, actually, I guess you could wait and decide tomorrow after you come back from fishing."

"That's no problem. I am not much of a shopper. I'll pass on the shopping trip.

"I can give you an extra key to the house so you can get in whenever they bring you home."

Richard called and set it up with Jacqueline that he would be ready at 6:00, he would help them clean fish, and they would all be there for fish dinner at 5:00 P.M.

Then Leit said, "Let's go into the kitchen and have some of Cassia's delicious mango dessert and either coffee, tea, or milk. Then I will tell you what I have in mind."

When they had all been served, Leit said, "Gloria and Richard, I know that you are here for important business and I do not want to detract from that in any way. But I also know that there is a great deal of beauty in Jamaica. I think that, by doing a little planning you can accomplish what you came to do and also enjoy yourself at the same time. I do not want to wear you out, so if I try to plan too much, please let me know."

"I thought for this Saturday I would give you a choice between two trips and then we might find time for the other one some time next week. We can either go to Montego Bay, which is beautiful and has several attractions, or Ocho Rios, which also has much to see. Either is about 40 to 45 miles away and would take about an hour each way. Depending on what I can line up tomorrow morning, if there should be some group available on Saturday we can work our trip around that. If you are open to it we can probably ask our church for the privilege of speaking for a few minutes at the close of our service on Sunday. I didn't ask if you both are church goers or not."

"Oh, yes, definitely. I've never been to a Seventh Day Adventist Church, however."

"No, Gloria, we are not Adventist. The school has that foundation, but we attend the Anglican Church in Mandeville."

"Well, we are also Anglican, so I am sure we will feel very much at home there. I was hoping that we could attend church while here."

"Now, I don't know if you two like to go to bed early or late. What I want to do is give you complete freedom of the house. Richard said he wanted to take a bath. There is a television in the living room. We have a tower but we just get one station here. There is a radio, including short wave and also a record player with records. Please make yourselves at home. There is one thing I wanted to show you, Gloria. It is our night sky. In London, with all of the lights and noise, you do not ever see the sky as it really is. I want to show you one of the best features of being in a place like Jamaica!"

"OK. I am ready when you are. We are not real night owls. We turn in, typically, around 10:00. But just so I save time for a shower before bed time, I am fine."

"Let's go to the front door, but close your eyes before we go out and don't open them again until I tell you to, OK?"

"OK, Leit."

Leit held Gloria's hand and guided her out through the door and down the steps. Gloria noted how gentle he was and that there was a bit of that "first time a boy held my hand" feeling about the moment. He guided her out to the front lawn. Then he said, "Now, look up and open your eyes!"

Gloria had a general idea of what to expect. She knew about the haze that is reflected in the sky in large cities,

A Message For All Time

and about the sounds that surround city dwellers that become so much a part of their lives that they totally lose awareness of the presence of the noise.

But she was totally unprepared for the experience that she was about to have. "Oh, it's....so..magnificent! It is as though we were on the inside of God! That doesn't sound quite right, but....I just don't have words.."

"I know. I know," whispered Leit.

"You said that 'people who get Jamaica's sand in their shoes never get it out'. I am beginning to feel that 'people who get Jamaica's stars in their eyes' might have the same trouble."

"Thank you, Gloria. I will remember that. I have never heard it said so beautifully before. Here is a bench. Would you like to sit for a while?"

"Yes. I guess this is the first time we have been alone. I had wanted to ask you if you had gone through the experience of losing a spouse."

"Yes. I lost my wife in child birth. I married a little later than some. By the time I had earned my doctorate I was almost 30. I came back here and met a young teacher at the school. She was a very sweet and talented person. We had been married for two years when we decided that it was time to start a family. She got an infection that could not

132

be reversed and she and the baby both died. I was absolutely devastated for a very long time. I never dated. I never had any interest in another woman until...well, I may be way out of line in saying this..."

There was a long pause. "Gloria, please forgive me if this offends you, but I feel a sort of transparency between us – as though there is no need to put up any kind of front. There is a chemistry between us that is quite unique. I have tried to call it "just a crush" and have tried to explain it away as my admiration for what you are trying to do for my family and the school. But I know that it is much more than that. I feel that, perhaps, God is giving me the possibility of another chance for family happiness. I am not unhappy. My work is very fulfilling. But it does not bring the joy that a husband and wife can have together. Now, I feel that, perhaps, I have said too much. I do not want to jeopardize our relationship, because it is so important that we work well together next week. "

"Leit. Let me start with your last statement and go from there. You have not jeopardized our relationship in any way. I have total respect for you as a person and as a man. We both know what a 'crush' is, and that it can be very powerful and very much like love. I must admit to your 'chemistry' statement. I feel it too. I also share your analysis that 'I am not unhappy but not really happy in the way that I know it can be'. What we have might be a crush. It might also be the beginning of real love. Only time can tell. During the war, few people had the luxury of 'time will tell'. Decisions had to be made quickly, right or wrong. Hopefully we do have time. I am very open to the possibility that God is giving both of us a second chance at family happiness. I am willing to test it with time.

I am not at all sorry that you had the courage to open the subject. I would probably have been too timid to do it. There was something that Jim Stark said in his message about freedom and tyranny having within them the seeds of their own destiny. I think that, perhaps, the same is true for true love. I believe that true love will have within it the seed of our knowing. I am willing to trust that, when that time comes for us to know, WE WILL KNOW. Now, I have a question. If I close my eyes, will you hold my hand and walk me back to the house?"

"I will be honored to, and you don't even have to close your eyes!"

Chapter 17. "A Team Is Born"

Friday morning was a "three way split". Jacqueline and her family came to pick up Richard. Leit was going to look through his list of possible contacts for the places where Gloria and Richard might be welcomed to share the "message". Gloria and Cassia planned to get better acquainted in the garden at the back of the house. But first there would be breakfast.

Of course, Richard would eat with Jacqueline's family. But what would Gloria have? The Jamaican breakfast varies according to the area. Some would eat eggs, bacon, and fried bread. But for others, breakfast is about the same as any other meal. You might have sweet potato pudding, boiled corn meal, boiled oats, salted mackerel, sardines, fried plantains, or beef liver. There are seasonal fruits and ackee, which some people say is a fruit, some say is a vegetable. Everyone drinks some sort of hot beverage – tea, herbal tea, or coffee. In Gloria's case, and since they were going to have fish for dinner, Cassia decided to have mostly what Gloria's stomach was used to: eggs, bacon, oatmeal, and as a Jamaican offering, a bit of mango and ackee.

When Jacqueline's family came for Richard, they were in a 1952 Pontiac. They were a happy family. They actually had a "welcome" song for Richard – something like a "happy birthday" song. Richard was so surprised. It really started the day off right.

Cassia fixed a pot of tea and she and Gloria went out to a comfortable lounge in the shade of a tropical tree. Cassia put the tea tray on a table and showed Gloria the large variety of flowers that grew, almost wild, in her back yard. There were tropical birds in the trees, talking among themselves.

"This is so beautiful,"said Gloria.

"One more selling feature of Jamaica", said Cassia. "I am beginning to think that a whole week here is going to be difficult to get over. The leaving is going to be nearly impossible.

"Well Gloria, let's sit down and I want to hear everything about life in London. Start when you were a little girl!"

Leit began to make a list of possible groups that might allow Gloria and Richard some time. They had already had a good reception by some of the students and faculty, but since school was not in session, a presentation to the whole school was not possible. He would contact several people on the school board and see if they would authorize calling an informal, voluntary assembly of the school in the school chapel for at least the local students and advertise it in the Monday newspaper. Then perhaps meet with the Board of Directors afterwards by themselves. Then there was the church to be called, the Education Committee of the government in Kingston, the people in charge of the concert tonight. We could advertise in the newspapers that we were available this week only, to speak to any civic group that had an interest in supporting a full University in Jamaica. Leit thought, "If only Richard and Gloria lived closer so that we could schedule groups for later!"

So the calling began, and that took the full morning for Leit. But when it was over, he was very pleased with what he had accomplished thus far.

At lunch time he announced the results to Gloria and Cassia. "We have an invitation to take 20 minutes of the service at church on Sunday. The concert tonight has given us all of the time we need up to 30 minutes. The Education Committee of the Government has invited us to a special called meeting of the Committee plus any interested Government officials on Thursday afternoon in Kingston. The Board of Directors of the School has called a meeting of the Board on Monday morning at 10:00 in order to have plenty of time to talk with you afterwards and then to have time to meet as a Board and make plans for going forward. Then they have authorized me to advertise in the papers for an assembly at the School chapel on Wednesday evening for all students, faculty, and all in the community who are interested. So, that is tonight, Sunday, Monday A.M.,Wednesday P.M., and Thursday afternoon. Pretty good for one morning of calling! That is five thus far and I believe there might be more as we move along."

As the trio sat, eating a lunch of delicious local greens and fresh fruit, Cassia said, "I have really enjoyed my time with Gloria. I asked her about growing up in London and, Leit, you will be amazed at what it was like for them during the war years. The kids would have to get up during the night and everyone would run to an air raid shelter when the sirens would blast. They would hear the bombs and wonder if the next one would hit right on top of them. It was certainly different for us wasn't it?"

"Yes, yes. The war was like in another world for us. We read about it and saw newsreels but it was hard to imagine what it was like. But, of course, Melvin got right into the thick of it.."

"I keep forgetting to ask," said, Gloria, "How did Melvin get involved with the Royal Navy? And, was he married?" "That is a very important question for you to ask, Gloria. Melvin was still young when he went to England. We had both just finished school. I had been teaching at the school for only one year, but he had been there for two years. A representative of the Royal Navy came to the school and presented the whole plan of dedicating the new cruiser, HMS Jamaica and that they needed to find some one who knew Jamaica and also was familiar with Navy life. They knew of no such person, so they wanted someone from our school who would be willing to experience Navy life for a few months to "get the flavor of it" before the dedication. Melvin was very quick to volunteer himself! He had no family beyond his parents, Cassia, and myself. My parents, of course, have passed away since that time. He was still rather young and had not found a life mate before that."

"Do you know of any close friends that we need to see personally?"

"He had many friends, Gloria, but I feel that our local meetings can take care of that."

When they had finished lunch, Leit said, "Now, if you girls are up to it, why don't we take a run up town, such as it is, and go into a few shops, pick up a few groceries, and see a few sights. We need not change clothes. Everyone looks very appropriate."

They all three got into the car after Leit opened the two passenger doors. Cassia insisted that Gloria sit in the front and she took the back seat. It only took about ten minutes to get to the shopping area. There was a pharmacy, a department store, a hardware store, and a restaurant in the first area. Cassia suggested that they begin with the department store. Gloria saw some sandals that she liked.

"Well, Leit, now I have sandals to get the sand into!" They all laughed. Gloria was surprised that it looked very much like a London department store. It was smaller over all, with smaller departments. It offered more types of items than a London store because there were no secondary stores to provide additional items, such as luggage shops, gift shops, etc.
After that they went into the pharmacy just to look around. It was pretty much limited to medical items. They did the

same with the hardware store. It had some items that would not be found in a London hardware store, such as bicycles, toys, fishing tackle and farming equipment. Then they got in the car and visited another shopping center that had a restaurant, a shop that sold crafts, and a small book store.

After about an hour they were ready to do some sight seeing. There were three main attractions that Leit wanted Gloria to see, the church that they would attend on Sunday, the Roxborough Great House, and an orchid sanctuary near town. They decided to go by the church, because they would be so busy there on Sunday and today they would be able to walk around and talk freely. The church was Marks Parish Church. It was built in 1814 and was the pride of Mandeville. It was a beautiful and historic brick building. They walked throughout and marveled at its beauty. They went outside and found many graves of antiquity that reflected the diversity of national origins of the early settlers. They read the markers and especially looked for the oldest.

After that they visited the Roxborough Great House, which was built in the late nineteenth century by Thomas Albert Manley, the father of one of Jamaica's historical heroes, the Rt. Hon. Norman Manley. They found many things that raised questions about Jamaica's history. Leit was very knowledgeable and tied everything together for Gloria. They then drove over to the orchid sanctuary, where the great variety of orchids and the expanse of color was just breathtaking. There were orchids of every hue in the rainbow. It was a nice way to finish their afternoon.

They almost forgot the groceries and doubled back to go for a few items that they needed for Sunday. The grocery store was not large but had more fresh items than she was used to seeing in London stores. Vegetables and fruits were quite different and this led to more questions for Leit to expound on. He purchased several things that he was not planning to get but wanted her and Richard to taste while they were in Jamaica.

By that time it was almost 3:00 and they knew that Richard would be coming home soon. They went home by a different route so that Gloria would see some other homes. When they got home, Gloria and Leit just relaxed with a cup of tea in the living room while they listened to an LP recording of Rachmaninoff's "Rhapsody on a Theme of Paganini". Cassia conveniently found something she needed to do in the back yard.

They were astonished at the sound, because high fidelity and stereo sound had just been introduced and this was Leit's first recording with those improvements.

"That is so beautiful, Leit!"

"Yes. It is one of my favorites," Gloria.
"Mine too. He is able to create so many emotions in me. And I can not exactly label them, like 'joy' or 'hope' or

'expectation', but the results are always so uplifting."

"Yes, Yes, rather like the stars in the Jamaican sky!" Teased Leit.

"Or like sand in my Jamaican sandals," laughed Gloria.

"We do have a lot in common, you and I," mused Leit.

"Yes, we do, and......"

"Hello, everybody! I'm back," yelled Richard.

"There comes the fisherman," said Gloria.

"And you could probably smell me from the street! Hey, when they say fish they aren't talking about those little minnows we catch at Brighton. These are monsters! I was cleaning fish that were twenty inches long. And were they fun to catch! They really put up a fight!"

"Did Jacqueline fish?" asked Leit.

Did she! She caught the biggest of the day! She knew just where to cast every time. She is really quite a girl."

So, I guess you had a good time?"

"Oh, my goodness. If we didn't accomplish another thing, that fishing trip was worth all that it took to get us here!"

"Well, let me tell you what we did this afternoon. Gloria gave a running account of all that they saw and showed Richard her new sandals and the gift orchid that she received at the orchid sanctuary."

"Isn't that Rachmaninoff?"

"Yes."

"Rhapsody on Paganini!"

"You are good! Richard."

"Well, it's one of my favorites, after all. But I've never heard a sound that wonderful from a record before."

"That is High Fidelity Stereophonic sound, Richard, the newest thing!"

"Well, gang, I don't want to be a spoil sport but we only have a few minutes to get ready to go to Jacqueline's so we had better get started."

Everyone dressed casually for supper and for the concert. Leit assured Gloria that no one ever dresses up for the Friday night concert.

The fish supper was outstanding. Mr. Rodriquez knew exactly how to bake the whole fish and there was more than they could possibly eat. There was a delicious bread that they eat with fish – a corn meal base. There was a beautiful salad and a fried patty made from ground up yucca root that was absolutely delicious. The Rodriquez family were just such good people and the fellowship so warm, that Gloria and Richard were sorry that the evening had to end so quickly. But they had to leave by 6:30 in order to get to the very important concert on time. The Rodriquez were coming just a bit later after they got the kitchen in order.

They arrived at the concert just five minutes before starting time. Many people spoke to Leit and Cassia as they came in but there was no time for conversation. Leit found his contact person and he showed them to four seats that were reserved down in front.

The lights dimmed and an announcer welcomed everyone and announced that next weeks offering would be a play called, "The Fox's Daughter" and it would be presented by a drama group from Kingston. Then he said, "Tonight we are very happy to have a group that has made several hit records and they make their home in Montego Bay. Please welcome the 'Wiggins' ".

{This might be a good place to just make an aside statement about Jamaican music in the 1950's. The most popular music, a forerunner of the sort of music that Bob Marley and the Wailers sang later, was called Mento. It was sometimes called Jamaican Calypso, but Calypso had more of a Spanish influence, whereas Mento had more of an African slave sound. It dealt with aspects of everyday life, often in a humorous way. It often included veiled sexual references. Harry Belafonte's song, "Day-O" (The Banana Boat Song) was a good example of Mento. The typical instrumentation for Mento was guitar, banjo, gourd shaker, and a large bass thumb piano, which was a large box that the player sat on and plucked tuned metal strips that gave off sounds.}

The first song that the Wiggins sang was "Maryan". It was well known from various recordings. The words were:

"ALL DAY ALL NIGHT MISS MARYAN,

DOWN BY THE SEA SHORE SIFTING SAND,

EVEN LITTLE CHILDREN LOVE MARYAN,

DOWN BY THE SEA SHORE SIFTING SAND."

The group sang several verses of that and received a good applause.

When they sang the next song, Leit looked at Gloria and they both laughed. It was called, "Run, Run, Run". The words were something like this:

"LOVE IS A COMMON ENEMY,

THE MOON AND THE STARS ARE ITS ARTILLARY .

WHEN THEY ATTACK YOU, YOU FIND THERE'S NO RETREAT,

AND YOU LOSE YOUR HEART UNLESS YOU USE YOUR FEET."

Chorus:

"RUN, RUN, RUN

WHEN YOU SEE A PRETTY WOMAN.

RUN, RUN, RUN, RUN LIKE YOU MAD,

WHEN YOU SEE A PRETTY WOMAN."

Another of their songs that was known around the world was, "Rum and Coca Cola".

"DRINKING RUM AND COCA COLA,

GO DOWN POINT KUMANNA,

BOTH MOTHER AND DAUGHTER,

WORKING FOR THE YANKEE DOLLAR."
When they sang the next song, Leit looked a little bit embarrassed as though he was "disowning it". It was

called, "Take Her To Jamaica".

"TAKE HER TO JAMAICA WHERE THE RUM
COMES FROM,

THE RUM COMES FROM, THE RUM COMES FROM,

TAKE HER TO JAMAICA WHERE THE RUM COMES
FROM,
AND YOU CAN HAVE SOME FUN".

Leit was rather hoping that the concert would end with a
more serious song to set the mood for the presentation, but
that was not going to happen. They were all funny and
light hearted. The gentleman that Leit had talked with then
went on the stage and said, "We hope that everyone has
enjoyed this wonderful group tonight and we hope that
they will come back soon. We have an unusual addition to
our program tonight. You all know Dr.Leit Dorster from
the West Indian School. He has two guests that he will
introduce. Folks, welcome Dr. Leit Dorster.

There was a thunderous applause that indicated that Leit
was greatly appreciated in Mandeville. "Thank you so
much, everyone! You all know about my brother, Melvin,
who disappeared while on a Royal Navy ship in 1942. I
want to introduce you to a boy and his mother, who have
flown all the way from London to share with us something
that they have learned about what actually happened on the
day that Melvin disappeared. Please welcome Mrs. Gloria

Parsons and her son, Richard.

There was another very robust applause as they came up on the stage. They all three quietly sat on three chairs that had been placed on central stage. Then, one by one they each gave their part of the story as they had done on the boat. At the end, Leit gave a very uplifting and challenging plan to work toward the building of a full University in Mandeville. When the presentation was finished, there was hardly a dry eye in the theater.

Before they finished Gloria said, "I would just like to make this one appeal. We have learned, just since we have been in Mandeville, that there does not seem to be anyone by the name Bob Swithers, the third sailor in the life boat, in the records of the Royal Navy. It is a high probability that his records were being transported on the ship that went down. So my appeal to you is, if you hear of anyone with that rather uncommon name or if you, perhaps, received any letters from Dr. Melvin Dorster that might have mentioned the name of Bob Swithers, please let us know. If we can even find out a city that he might have been from, it would be a beginning. You might be helping us locate someone, somewhere, who needs to know what happened to their missing loved one. Thank you very much!"

When Gloria finished, there was a standing ovation that went on for five minutes. The evening was a wonderful indication that the dream of Melvin Dorster was soon to become a reality.

Chapter 18. "Temporary Tourists".

When they all returned home from the concert, the telephone rang. "Please excuse me for calling this late, Dr. Dorster. I would have contacted you at the concert but I had to call someone first. I am from Christiana, about 18 miles from Mandeville, and we are having a High School Festival tomorrow. There will be students, parents, faculty, and friends there. We are expecting at least 800 people. Would it be possible, with such short notice, for the three of you to make a presentation like you did tonight at about 8:30? We begin the Festival at 3:00 with all sorts of games and activities, then supper at 6:00, a talent show at 7:00, and your part would follow the talent show at about 8:30. You could come as early as you wish or wait until almost 8:30 to arrive if that is better for you. And we would be delighted to have you as our guests for supper if that is convenient. I heard your presentation last night and would so like for my folks to hear it."

"Thank you, and your name is.....?"

"Oh, I'm sorry, I'm Donna Bowling. I am the President of the Parents' Association, and I did call the Principal of the High School to be sure that it is OK."

"Mrs. Bowling, I feel sure that we can do that but just let me check with Mrs. Parsons and Richard just to make double sure." Leit relayed the message to Gloria and Richard and they shook their heads vigorously. "Yes, Mrs.

Bowling. They said that they will be delighted to do that. Thank you!"

"Well, that is another really good contact for us. We have had several fine students from Christiana. They usually have about 30 graduates from high school every year. They would benefit greatly from having a University in Mandeville. Now, who would like some refreshments while we discuss tomorrow?"

The quartette enjoyed hot tea and demolished a chocolate cake while deciding to go to Montego Bay in the morning. "So, we will wake you in the morning at 6:30, eat breakfast at 7:30, and leave at 8:30. How is that?"

Gloria and Richard both agreed.

In the morning, Gloria and Richard alternated in showering and getting dressed. They all had a full breakfast of eggs, sausage, baked beans, and fried bread, with coffee and a sweet roll on the side.

"I think I will gain 10 pounds this week," lamented Gloria.

"You can stand it, Gloria," encouraged Cassia.

They all dressed casual and took bathing suits along. "just in case".

They arrived in Montego Bay at 10:00 and decided to start

at Belvedere Estate, one of the first sugar cane plantations in Jamaica. After that they went to one of the largest shopping areas that Gloria had ever seen. It had clothing shops for men and women, leather goods - shoes, hand bags, jackets, and gloves. There was a large crafts "barn", with woven baskets, carved wooden bowls and other objects, and sewn objects - jackets, gloves and hats.

They then went to Bay Roc, where Humphrey Bogart and Lauren Bacall came to play.
They visited Lucea, a small town near Montego Bay, where the remains of a 17th century fort were still visible.

They had a fabulous lunch at one of the famous Montego Bay restaurants that featured Jerk chicken.

After lunch, they went to a lake that had advertised "pedal boats". They decided that it would be prudent to change into their swim suits before trying out the boats. Each boat had a comfortable bench seat with a canvas cover overhead to protect from the sun. There were two sets of foot pedals, similar to those on a bicycle. The boat was propelled and steered by the speed of the pedaling. Both occupants pedaled.

Gloria and Leit got into one boat and Cassia and Richard got into another. They did not anticipate the benefit that would develop from this decision, but the private time between Gloria and Leit and between Cassia and Richard turned out to be of great importance to everyone involved.

At first they played games of circling or attempted "ramming" but soon each went their separate ways.

As Gloria and Leit began to pedal, they both pedaled rapidly, since they were both used to bicycling. Then Gloria began to giggle. "It looks like we are racing and neither one is gaining on the other!"

"You're right," said Leit. "Let's slow down and head for the little platform out in the middle of the lake."

When they arrived at the platform there was a place to tie the boat and stairs to go up. They found a covered bench swing on the platform and sat there. "This is so pleasant, Leit," said Gloria.
"I can't think of any place in the whole world that I would rather be than right here, right now, with you Gloria!"

"I haven't heard you say what you studied for your doctorate, Leit. I heard you say that Melvin was in Political Science."

"I did my undergaduate work in Philosophy, Gloria, and did my doctorate in the area of Philosophy of Religion."

"And so, what do you teach at the school?"

"I am head of the Theology School. There are just three teachers in the Theology School and we divide up the teaching duties equally among us."

"I am going to expose my ignorance, Leit, but I trust you enough to do that. I know that 'one's philosophy of life' means how a person approaches life or what he believes about how to live life - am I right so far?"

"You are right on target!"

"OK. So, how would you major on that in college?"

"A good question, Gloria. If a person wants to learn how to build a house, he might go with a builder and watch him build and learn from that. But, if he does not know any builders he might get a good bit of knowledge from reading manuals that some builders have written. In the same way, if a person wants to learn how to live life in the most effective way, he might live along side some successful people for a number of years. But that would be very difficult to arrange.

"Yet there have been many succcessful men and women who have written their manuals on this subject. These are called Philosophy Books, and the library is full of them. They are not all of equal value and therefore the student of life must read them and decide what makes sense in his own experience. Down through the ages men like Plato and Aristotle and Kierkegaard and Thoreau and hundreds of others have written their 'manuals'. Then what I do is help students to understand what these Philosophers were trying to say.

"What I tried to do in my Doctoral work was to put together what these Philosophers said and what the Religious leaders through out history have said and try to see where they seem to fit together. But the whole point is to help people get a better grasp on the best way to live their lives."

"Leit, that is so important! I wish that I had been offered that sort of help when I was in high school. I would have absorbed that like a sponge. I absolutely longed for help in that area when I was 17. Actually, that is exactly where Richard is right now! Do the students seem to appreciate it?"

"By and large they do. We have one or two 'required courses' that are looked at, I think, as a 'chore'. But the students who choose to study Theology are well motivated and seem to want more. That is one reason I want to see a four year university in Mandeville."

"Not to change the subject, Gloria, but you said that you do not have strong ties in London, other than your job. What about Richard. I am sure you know what I would wish for if I were blowing out my candles on a birthday cake. I wake up thinking of the fact that I might never see you again after this Friday. Just imagine, for a moment, that my wishes could come true and you were to come and live here in Jamaica, would Richard be able to be happy here, or is his life so much a part of London that he would never consider coming here permanently."

"Is this a proposal, Leit?" Gloria said it as a whimsical tease, but was sorry immediately.

Leit looked at Gloria with a quizical look on his face. "Well,no. I mean, if I thought it had even a chance, then, yes! I mean I hadn't meant for it to be because I would have thought it was too early, but , yes! Since the cat is out of the bag, Yes! I'll claim that cat as mine!"

"I'm sorry, Leit. I didn't mean to embarrass you. It was very unfair of me. I should not have treated it so lightly. I think this whole, wonderful day has made me a little giddy. I do think that there is a part of me that wants a proposal from you, or I never would have said what I did. But I would never want you to propose to me unless you were totally ready. And I am just enough of a 'purist' that I would want to hear the best and most well thought out proposal that you are capable of. Why don't we just call this a 'false start' that was not the fault of the runner but of the person who 'fired the starter gun' too soon. That was me, of course. As I said, Leit, couples had to make decisions quickly like that during the war. Some worked out well and some did not. But we are not in that position now. Let's give it more time. Let me say, though, that I also wake up thinking that I might not see you again after Friday. That is not a good feeling for me either. Will you please forgive me for what I just did to you?"

"There is nothing to forgive, Gloria. I am very glad that it happened just as it did. Now I do not have to wonder if you know how serious my intentions are. I know that you know!"

Meanwhile, on another part of the lake, Cassia and Richard have pedaled their boat to a little man made island and have pulled their boat up on the sand. "Oh, that was such fun, Richard. You must be quite an athlete in school, because it was all I could do to keep up with you and you looked as though you were hardly working."

"I play a little soccer. But you were going pretty good too, I think!"

"It's good to rest a while though. Come tell me about yourself, Richard. Have your interests begun to solidify yet? Do you know what you would like to shoot for after high school?"

Richard was quiet for about 30 seconds while he put together his words in his mind. "Miss Dorster..."

"Oh, I can't take that from you, Richard. I know you too well in this short time for you to be saying Miss Dorster. But I know that you have been taught to show respect, so I guess, 'Cassia' is out of the question. Could you bring yourself to say, 'Aunt Cassia' and I would explain our choice to Leit and Gloria?"

"You know, I have always felt a little 'short changed' not to have an aunt. Mom and Dad had no sisters. So, yes, if you will tell Mom and Dr. Dorster, so they won't laugh at me, I will go with 'Aunt Cassia' ".

"So, here we go. I'll ask the question again. Do you know what career or goal you will be shooting for when you finish high school?"

"You just asked two different things, 'Aunt Cassia' -Ha Ha, I did get the words out! Any way - two different things. My goal I know already and I have had the same goal since I was 12 years old. I want to be the best person I am capable of being, and that, to me, means trying to please God in all that I do. Now, as to my career, I suppose this might change over time but I really want to train to be a teacher. I have had several teachers that have helped me in so many ways, especially since my Dad died. I want to be able to be that sort of teacher. And you know what! You are the first person, other than my Mom, to ever ask me that question, and I thank you for it! I think it did me a lot of good to tell somebody what my thoughts are about a career - that is, to actually put it into words."

"Well, Richard, you have just given me one of the highest honors that I have ever received. I feel that you are already becoming 'that sort of teacher'. I don't know when I have ever felt better in my whole life than I feel right this minute."

"Thank you, Aunt Cassia. I feel about that same way myself! - I think I see a foreign pedal boat coming this way and I'll bet someone will yell 'Time to go!' "

"Hey, Richard and Cassia. I guess it is time to go if we are going to make it back in time for the program tonight. We might as well try to get there for supper and then watch the talent show!"

"OK, Richard. Looks like you were right about what would be yelled," laughed Cassia.

Chapter 19. "A Revelation".

They had not planned to go home before the Festival in Christiana, since that town is between Montego Bay and Mandeville. So the ladies just planned to repair their makeup in the rest room at the school. They had, of course, showered and dressed again after swimming in the lake.

They asked for Mrs. Bowling when they got to the school and she was a delightful hostess. She was impressed by what she had heard at the concert and was genuinely grateful that they had come to the Festival.

They were just in time for supper and it was a buffet in which a committee of parents had brought their favorite dishes. In fact, the Parents Association had printed a School Recipe Book the year before and the goal was to have every recipe in the book duplicated at the Festival. Our quartet was convinced that they had met that goal when they saw the loaded tables.

The Talent Show was equally well done. There was a theme that was built around well known movies, and each entry in the Talent Show was required to relate their song, dance, or whatever other talent they presented to a particular movie. It could be a song from the movie or it could be related to the title or to the name of an actress in the movie, etc. So there was a great deal of imagination and ingenuity used in the choice of acts.

One movie that was used, for instance, was Dr. Jekyll and Mr. Hyde. Two young men dressed as the two characters in the movie and they sang "Friendship, Friendship, just a perfect blendship. When other friendships are all forgot, ours will still be hot!" It brought the house down!

At the conclusion of the show, Mrs. Bowling came on the stage and said, "Dear friends, I heard something last night that so touched my heart that I really hated that all of my friends in Christiana were missing the wonderful experience that I was having. So I called the folks that were involved and they generously agreed to present it for you just as I heard it last night. I am more grateful to them than I can possibly say. You will know why when you have heard them. So, without further ado, I present Dr. Leitman Dorster, Head of the School of Theology of the West Indian Training School. He will introduce his two friends."

They did present everything exactly as the night before and, again, there was a very warm and heartfelt response from all ages that were in the audience. They did allow a period of questions, and the usual questions were asked about their life in London, their trip to Jamaica, and their plans after Jamaica. Gloria then presented her special appeal concerning Bob Swithers, but there were no responses, either at the concert or tonight, concerning any information about Bob Swithers. Again, as with the night before, Leit made his special appeal for everyone to please give their support when plans were unveiled concerning a four year university Program. Several seniors at the high school talked with Dr. Dorster afterwards, concerning their entrance into the West Indian Training School. All in all it was a very successful evening.

On the way back to Mandeville, Leit said, "Of course it is too early to really approach the question, Gloria, but what will you do if you go all week with no results concerning Bob Swithers?"

"Well," said Gloria, "Sir Thomas is continuing to look in the Naval Records. I suppose if nothing comes from our audience or from the records, I will just be listening for that name to be mentioned somewhere for the rest of my life. Our quest will never be over until it is over."

"That's the way I feel too," added Richard.

"Well, that must be contagious because that is the way I feel too," said Leit.

"Me too," joined Cassia.

"Sounds unanimous to me," laughed Gloria. "But let's feel positive about it. I think there is a good chance that someone, somewhere, will give us a clue!"
"I do hope so," said Leit..

When they got home it was quite late. "Anyone want a bath tonight or do you want to wait until in the morning?"

Everyone said, "Tomorrow!" Anyone want some refreshments before bed?" Again, everyone said, "Not for me!"

"OK. Church is at 10:30. We usually eat a leisurely breakfast at 8:30. So is everyone OK with a 7:30 wake up call?"

"I would prefer 7:00." said Gloria.

"Me too," echoed Richard.

"OK, good night. I have really enjoyed today! Thank you all!" said Leit.
"It has been one of my best fun days ever," said Gloria.

"And I enjoyed boating with Aunt Cassia", said Richard.

"Aunt?" said Leit.

"Sorry, Richard. Haven't had a chance to do my duty yet!"

"Forgiven," laughed Richard.

The next morning they had a light breakfast of oat meal, sweet rolls, and coffee. Then Cassia invited Gloria in to her closet to choose and try on several dresses. She did find one that looked really nice on her. Cassia said, "Gloria, you just inherited a new dress, because that has never looked that good on me!"

Gloria said, "Thanks Cassia, I love it!"

Leit said, "Richard, could I interest you in looking through my things? You are quite welcome!"

"I think I am OK for today, Dr. Dorster. I assume they allow a sport shirt on someone my age."

"Oh, none of the students wear ties anywhere in Jamaica, Richard. You are going to look fine. I did notice that you have a beautiful white Guayabera shirt. That would be the perfect choice."

"That it is, then!" said Richard.

They arrived at the church and Leit said,"OK, just so you will know. Most people do bow to the altar when they enter. We use the Book of Common Prayer, rather than the Book of Alternative Services. And we use the Apostles' Creed rather than the Nicene Creed. That's about it. You should feel pretty much at home. The Priest is a young man, somewhat casual – I think you will like him very much!"

"I'm sure I will," said Gloria.

The worship service was very much like Gloria was used to in London. The sermon was on Jesus' parables of the Lost Coin, the Lost Sheep, and the Prodigal Son. It affirmed the fact that things that are valuable are well worth the extra effort required. Gloria applied that truth to their own search. After the sermon the Priest said, "Dr. Dorster has guests with us today and they have enriched our worship by their presence. They would like to share something with us that is very important to them and when you have heard them, I think you will agree that it is very important to us also." With that introduction, Leit stood and introduced Richard and Gloria and they made their presentation as before. Leit noted, later, that everybody's part seemed to be improving as practice refined their delivery. The response of the church people was very positive, and several of their comments were along the lines of "We loved having you and we really wish that you were living here among us!" Gloria thought, "more sand in my shoes, indeed!"

When they returned home, Gloria asked Leit to please set up a long distance call to Sir Thomas for her. She called him dutifully and apologized for it being so late – 7:00 P.M. London time. She reported on the good response Friday night, the trip to Montego Bay, the good contacts at the school in Christiana, and the excellent experience they had just enjoyed at Church. Thom commented that it had been just five days but that it seemed to him like two weeks. Gloria let that go by without a comment, because to her the time was passing much too quickly and she found herself wishing that she could stay the whole summer.

After lunch, Leit said that there was a soccer game in town at the local ball field at 3:00 and wondered if anyone was interested. Cassia said, "Why don't you three run along and give me time to do some chores around the house that have suffered from my absence on Friday and yesterday?"

Leit said, "What do you feel about that, you two?"

"Sounds like fun to me!" said Gloria.
"Me too," echoed Richard.

"Good! Casual clothes! Do you need to peek at Cassia's wardrobe, Gloria?"

"No. I think I'm still OK," said Gloria.

"I still have some things too," added Richard.

The soccer game was especially enjoyable for Richard because the Jamaicans seemed to attack the game with just a little bit different flavor than the British, and he made some comments along from his observations. Gloria had to ask Leit several questions because she was not a regular soccer fan, beyond a few games that she had watched when Richard was playing.

After supper they watched a favorite drama series that Leit and Cassia watched with the same enthusiasm that many people maintain for their favorite "soap opera". Gloria observed, "We do not get this program in London and what a shame that is! It is such a lovely and well done piece. I shall certainly hate not seeing what happens when

Betty finds out about Benjamin losing his job."

"Well, of course we know that there is a remedy for that, don't we?"teased Leit.

"Did I miss somethings? I don't follow you," quizzed Richard.

"Oh, Dr. Dorster has wished, on several occasions, that you and I lived in Mandeville instead of London.!"

"What a coincidence. I have wished the same thing!" laughed Richard.

Leit and Gloria looked at each other. "Are you serious, Richard," asked his mother, hardly believing her own hearing.

"Of course I know that it isn't possible, with your job and all, but I would move here in a minute if the choice was mine to make."

"Well, I am so glad that you expressed your feelings about that, Richard, because I had absolutely no idea that you felt that way!"

"Mom, I've felt like that ever since the sail boat trip, maybe all the way back to when we got off of the plane and I smelled the whole different air that they breathe in Jamaica."

Well, now, Gloria had a whole new set of conditions and possibilities to ponder tonight when her head hit her pillow.

"Let's think about tomorrow everyone. We have a meeting at 10:00 with the Board of Directors of the school tomorrow. That should take until almost lunch time. Then, Cassia has a proposition for Gloria"

"Oh, Yes, Gloria. The school has a weekly session, during the summer time, with a group of young girls from very poor families. We meet with them to teach them home making skills. It is really sad to see how very little they know about the simplest things that you and I learned from our mothers about house keeping. They just do not have a clue about cleanliness, cooking, money management, manners, etc. So we meet with these girls every Monday afternoon from 2:00 until 4:30 in the kitchen of the school. Would you be interested in observing that with me tomorrow, Gloria?"

"Oh, Yes. That sounds like something I would be very interested in learning about. Thank you, Cassia. Count me in!"

"OK, that leaves me and Richard. Have you done any snorkeling, Richard?"

"I've heard of it and have seen it in the movies, but I have never done it myself."

"Well, down the beach from where we tie up our boat, there is a little shack where they rent snorkeling gear – foot fins, masks, and snorkel tubes. There is a sunken airplane near there and with the assortment of fish that range in and out of that airplane, it really is something to see! Would you like to try that while your mother and 'Aunt Cassia' go to their meeting?"

"That sounds like something that's almost too great to wish for! Yes! Let's do it!"

They went to bed on Sunday night with questions of the future dancing in Gloria's head, visions of the joy of first time snorkeling filling Richard's head, and a possibility almost too wonderful to dream about, keeping Dr. Leitman Dorster awake for the better part of the night.

Chapter 20. "A Little Child Shall Lead Them"

Gloria awoke with a start. It was Monday morning. Her emotions were definitely mixed. She was looking forward to the visit with the girls at the school. But she was counting and she knew that there were only four days left in Jamaica. Of those, only three would be spent in Mandeville, which she had begun to love. How could she leave this place, these people, this family, this...She heard Cassia stirring in the kitchen. She turned over and saw that Richard was already awake, staring at the ceiling. "Good morning, Sweetie, what are you thinking about?"

"Well, two things, Mom. I'm thinking about how much fun I'm going to have snorkeling. Then, how important that meeting is with the Board of Directors this morning, and...I guess I should have said three things. Do you realize that we have only three more days left in Mandeville? I need to call Jacqueline. She asked me to let her know when I would have some time to come over there."

"Why don't you ask Leit this morning about this evening. I don't think we have anything tonight. You could call her after breakfast."

"Yes, that's what I will do. Thanks Mom, you're a jewel!"

"I know better, but I'll accept all erroneous compliments! Now, do you want the first shower or the extra time in bed?"

"I'll do the shower."

Gloria spent the few extra minutes thinking about Leit – the premature gray hair, wavy and thick. His eyes that fix upon you when you speak, as though you were saying the most important thing in the world. His kindness, his intelligence, just him!

Richard was back before she expected him. She took her turn and dressed quickly.

Breakfast was full, with eggs and sausage, waffles on the side. Coffee and tea as always, and some fresh mango.

Richard mentioned about the possibility of going to the Rodriquez home for the evening. Leit said that the evening was free and that he was welcome to use the Nash if he wanted to. Richard thanked him and was surprised but grateful that Leit had that much confidence in him. He called Jacqueline and they made a date for 6:30 for him to come to supper.

The meeting with the Board of Directors began with some misunderstanding on the part of a few members. There were two or three who thought that the attempt to build a four year university was to be another institution in competition with West Indian Training School. They had already decided among themselves to fight against the whole concept. But, after hearing the story of "the message" and being assured that any final institution that would come about in the future would be a direct outgrowth of the West Indian School, the Board voted unanimously and enthusiastically to participate in the planning for and launching of a foundation for the new university in Mandeville.

The Board also voted to put two bronze memorial plates in prominent places. One would read: "I BELIEVE THAT FREEDOM WILL WIN OVER TYRANNY WHEREVER THE TWO MAY MEET. FREEDOM HAS WITHIN IT'S OWN SEED THE FRUIT OF TRIUMPH, AND TYRANNY, LIKEWISE, HAS WITHIN IT'S SEED THE FRUIT OF FAILURE. GOD AND THE NATURE OF LIFE WILL SEE TO THAT."Jim Stark, March 1942.

The other memorial plate will read: "IT HAS BEEN A PROFOUND GIFT TO ME, AS A CITIZEN OF JAMAICA, TO HAVE HAD THE PRIVILEGE OF KNOWING YOUNG MEN AND WOMEN WHO ARE SERVING SO BRAVELY IN THIS WAR. I THINK OF THEIR COURAGE AND THEIR SINCERE DEVOTION TO COUNTRY, TO FREEDOM, TO GOD, AND TO TRUTH. BUT THIS WAR WILL NOT LAST FOREVER. THESE YOUNG MEN AND WOMEN WILL COME HOME AND WILL NEED TO FIND SCHOOLS THAT ARE CAPABLE OF NOURISHING THEIR GOOD MINDS, SCHOOLS THAT WILL RECEIVE THEM WITH OPEN ARMS. I, FOR ONE,HAVE BEEN GIVEN A NEW VISION OF THE NEED FOR THESE SCHOOLS TO HAVE THE VERY HIGHEST STANDARDS AND GOALS. AS A PERSON WHO HAS

SOME INFLUENCE IN SUCH A SCHOOL, I PLAN TO
GO BACK TO JAMAICA AND HELP TO ESTABLISH
ONE OF THE FINEST UNIVERSITIES IN THE
WESTERN HEMISPERE. WITH GOD'S HELP AND
THE HELP OF MY FELLOW COUNTRYMEN, IT
WILL HAPPEN!" Dr. Melvin Dorster, Royal Navy of
England and citizen of Jamaica.

Leit, Gloria, and Richard were very pleased with this
response from the Board. The Board also established a
Task Force for drawing up the overall plans for developing
a full university program.

After the meeting they ate a light lunch at the Bloomfield
Great House Restaurant and enjoyed seeing Lou and Luigi
again.

Richard and Leit had brought their towels and bathing suits
with them. They took Cassia and Gloria by the school and
went on to the shore for snorkeling. The weather was
perfect – not too hot but just right. They went to the
Snorkel Shack and got two sets of everything they needed.
The sunken airplane was about 50 yards out under a
marker. They pulled a small raft for use if they needed to
rest. They tied that to the marker. There were five or six
other snorkelers in the area – all having a glorious time.

Richard was just beside himself from all that he saw. There
were several large Rays gliding leisurely below, he saw
various schools of fish, all in magical colors. There was

one scuba diver on the very bottom, swimming in and out of the various openings of the old airplane. Leit and Richard made several deep dives but were unable to reach the extreme depth of the wreckage. But Richard was obviously having the time of his life. His bond with Dr. Dorster was growing stronger as a result of this experience.

Meanwhile, Gloria was enjoying herself just as much with her activity. She observed at first but after thirty minutes she was assigned to work with two girls – Gabriel, called Gabi, and Consuela. Gabi was very cautious and hesitant to trust a stranger, but Consuela was just the opposite. She could not get close enough to Gloria. Gloria was helping these two girls to know how to use a kitchen stove safely – what settings to use for different purposes, like boiling water or slow cooking soup or cooking meat in the oven. Gloria was enjoying doing the sort of things that she had not been able to do just having a son and no daughters.

When she anticipated coming to this group, she saw it as a way to give of herself, but she never expected to actually enjoy the process - not this much, any way. It was as if she were finding a niche in a place that she would never have thought to look. She thought, "If only those other realtors could see me now!"

Cassia was quietly enjoying the obvious bliss that Gloria was experiencing. She knew that Leit would be glad that it was a good day for Gloria.

They had planned to go home with another worker who lived close to the Dorsters. They knew that Leit and Richard would likely be later than 4:30 getting back. But when it was time for the girls to leave, Gabi did not want to leave Gloria. Somehow she had found in Gloria a source of friendship and security that she had never experienced before. She said, "Ms. Gloria, I will be with you next time too, OK?"

Gloria said, "Honey, I am just here for this week. Then I must go to London, in England, far, far away."

"But you will be back with Gabi the next week, OK?"
"Gabi, I don't think I will ever....Dear, I am not sure if I will ever....I don't know, Gabi. We will see, OK?"

"OK, Gabi will see you coming back to Gabi in Jamaica. That is what Gabi will see, OK?"

Gloria gave Gabi a hug but tried to hide the tears that were covering her face. She almost cried audibly when she heard, "Gabi not want you to be sad! Be happy like Gabi is because I found Ms. Gloria!"

Cassia watched the conversation from the doorway and just shook her head. She sensed the emotions that were flooding over Gloria.

They both waited quietly for the neighbor to go get her car to pick them up. "I'm sorry, Gloria, if this was the wrong thing to involve you in. I had no intention of making you sad, please believe me."

"Dear Cassia. Tears are sometimes a necessary vehicle for decision making. If nothing had touched me today, the morning would merely have been an interesting experience that I would have filed away somewhere in my memory. But instead, because a little girl touched my heart, this experience today will be a part of one of the most important decisions I will make in my life time."

Cassia hugged Gloria, but did not ask her to elaborate on what she meant. She knew. She knew.

The neighbor asked, "Well, how did you like our class, Mrs. Parsons?"

"It was just great, Mrs. Palmer. I am so glad I came with Cassia. You are doing wonderful things with these girls." Gloria was doing everything she could to cover up the emotional impact that she was living through at that moment.

When Gloria got home she said, "Cassia, how about giving me about 30 minutes to just be by myself. I just need to process the experience I had with little Gabi. OK?" "Gloria, I heard enough to know that she was asking for the impossible and I think she made you ask yourself if it was really the impossible or not. Am I getting close?"

"You hit it right on the head, Cassia. So you know why I have some thinking to do. You also know that Richard has already declared his preference. Cassia, I don't mean to put an unfair burden on you but I respect your judgment. If you have any wisdom to share at this point, I am very open to any help you can give."

"Dear Gloria. I am not one to meddle in other folks affairs, but you have asked me and I will tell you as I see it. In the short time that I have been with you I feel that you are almost like a sister to me. I know that Leit is certainly impressed with you, I would say that he is in love with you, but that is for him to say. He certainly has not experienced anything like this since his wife died. You seem to have succumbed, rather quickly, to the subtle power that Jamaica has had on all of us who live here. We have heard, as you said, what Richard would choose if the decision were his. So, Dear Friend of mine, it all boils down to what you are feeling down deep in your heart."

"If it were left up to me, I would say, 'go and wrap up all of the loose ends with your Message project, close all of your business in London, and come back to Jamaica. Let your 'heart business' with Leit take it's course whether it takes a week or a year. If you go back to your 'business as usual' existence in London you will wonder, for the rest of your life, if you had forfeited your chance for a greater happiness"

"And, just so that you will know, my living with Leit has

been a temporary convenience because I sold my former house where I lived alone quite happily. So, if you come back to Jamaica, one of your first assignments might well be to help me find another house. Now, Gloria – you asked my opinion and I think that I have given it rather candidly but sincerely. If it sounds a bit overly simplistic then just remember that I am an incurable romantic at heart. I do thank you for asking."

Gloria's only response was to hug her very close and say, "Thank you! Thank you! You are a friend and you are like my sister. You have helped me more than you can ever know. Now let me take some time to collect myself before Leit and Richard get home."

Chapter 21. "A Decision Is Made".

Gloria realized that she had let another day slip by without calling Thom Lawn. What caused her a problem with this was the six hour difference in time between London and Jamaica. She was home on Monday by 5:00 P.M. But it was already 11:00 in London. Thom would not have minded at all but it just did not seem right to her, somehow, to call anyone that late at night.

Richard came in at about 5:15 and he was absolutely ecstatic over his snorkeling experience. He didn't have much time to get ready for his date with Jacqueline, so he talked very rapidly - "Mom, the Sting Rays were at least four feet across, and those pretty little fish were in schools of at least a hundred each! They all moved as one body. It was remarkable to see. That scuba diver – he was way down on the bottom of the ocean where the plane was. It was amazing!"

"Gloria looked at Leit and said, "Thank you, Leit! That will be a high light of his whole summer. It was such a good idea!"

"I enjoyed it just as much as he did. He really is a good young man! You have done a fine job with him. You can be very proud."

"Thank you, Leit."

"Well, ladies, since we have all gotten home late and Richard is going out for dinner, what if I run to town and pick up a package of fish and chips – or would you want to go over to McPhee's and sit at an outdoor table and eat fish and chips?"

"Well, Leit, you know the answer to that. I am always ready to go to McPhee's – my favorite place in the whole universe! And I think it would be a shame to let Gloria get away from Jamaica without going there at least once. Besides, one time and she will be hooked and maybe that will cause her to come back to Jamaica some day."

"Then that is definitely what we ought to do for sure!" laughed Leit. "So, we all go as we are – 'barefooted or dressed in tux. McPhee doesn't care!' "

When they got to McPhee's, Gloria could not believe her eyes. It was like a huge bamboo hut with a thatched roof. The smells of broiling fish and charcoal were so tantalizing. When they went inside, there were pretty girls in grass skirts and young native men in authentic costumes and they placed a Hawaiian Lei on each guest with a smile and a happy "Aloha!"greeting. The food was as good as Gloria had ever tasted anywhere. It truly was a memorable evening.

After they had been there for about thirty minutes, it was time for a floor show. Four girls and four young men danced out into an open area of the restaurant. They were accompanied with two young men playing native drums. Leit had chosen the table well, as they were directly next to the dancers.

The dancers immediately went into a spirited dance that was absolutely electric. Then the men went off the floor and the girls did a traditional hula dance in which their hands told a story of love. After that the men came back on with different costumes, obviously decked out with weapons. They did a special war dance that would have impressed the most vicious enemy. Then the girls came back on with a different story to be told with their lovely hula hands. Lastly, the men came back and did what was obviously a dance of love and mating but which was in very good taste. "This is just like being in Hawaii" thought Gloria, though she had never been there.

Gloria talked about the details of the evening all the way home. She said, "Now I understand what Cassia meant when she said, 'Gloria will be hooked'."
When they got home they just sat around the living room for a few minutes, relaxing. Leit put a record on the player and said, "For an A+, who can tell me what this is?"

"Get out your A+, Leit," said Gloria. Anyone from England would be ashamed not to recognize 'Fantasia On a Theme by Thomas Tallis, by Ralph Vaughan Williams'. I think that it has some of the most beautiful chord progressions ever written."

"You are very good in music, Gloria. I'll wager you are being modest about 'everyone in England recognizing that'. Do you play an instrument?"

I play the piano passably – not concert quality by any means, and I played Oboe in the high school orchestra. I sometimes miss that!"

"Just out of curiosity, try this one, 'for added credit to your A+' " laughed Leit. He put on another record from a different album. The music was obviously from another period.

Gloria listened to three chords and said, "Eine Kleine Nactmusick, by Mozart. But that one is too easy, so I would feel guilty accepting extra credit for that!"

"You're out of my league," laughed Cassia. "I do well to recognize 'The Banana Boat Song'!"

"Well, not to change the subject, but tomorrow is a free day as far as our commitments are concerned. I said something earlier about going to Ocho Rios while you are here. What is your thinking, girls?"

"Actually, Leit, I could enjoy a 'stay at home' day. I don't want to be a spoil sport, but I would really like to just walk the neighborhood or see a little more of Mandeville if it is OK with you two."

"I think I would like that too," replied Cassia, and there is another shopping center that Gloria did not see on Friday."

"That sounds fine to me," said Leit. It is quite possible that Richard might want to have one more visit with Jacqueline. There seems to be more than a little interest there from both directions."

Richard got in at about 10:00 and was full of how much fun Jacqueline and her family are and that they wanted to know if he was available any time tomorrow for a picnic? Leit advised that the whole day was free and that the rest of them were going to stay near home or go up town briefly at the most. He suggested that he call Jacqueline right then and make plans. He did call and they said they would pick him up at 11:00 in the morning. Everyone turned in before 11:00 P.M.

After breakfast the next morning, Gloria said to Richard, "How about a walk up that hill in back of the house, Richard? Are you up to it?"

"I've been wondering how much of Mandeville we could see from up there, Mom, Sure! Ten minutes?"
"Ten minutes!"

As they got to the bottom of the grassy hill, Gloria took off running as a challenge. Richard caught her rather quickly and they laughed together. Richard took his Mom's hand and they walked , swinging hands, and reached the top in

five minutes. Gloria sat looking towards town. "OK,
Sweetie, I need some input. How do you see us? What is
happening here? Are we in a fantasy or is this whole thing
real? Bottom line – can you see us living here or is this a
crazy dream we are having?"

"Mom, in a way it is crazy, but I think that sometimes
people find themselves in situations that they did not know
were coming and they are forced to make a quick decision.
But just because it is a quick decision that doesn't make it a
bad decision. I honestly think that God has given us a
beautiful gift – an unexpected gift. I really think that a
whole life of happiness is being offered here. I think we
should take it. I am assuming that you mean 'staying in
Mandeville'."
"Yes, and it really hit me right in the face yesterday
afternoon." Gloria told Richard about her conversation
with Gabi. "Another question is, what do you think about
Leit, Honey? Could you see me marrying again – that is,
marrying Leit?"

"Mom, I know you loved Dad, there is no doubt about it.
But I have watched you with Dr. Dorster and he really
lights you up all over! I can see you being really happy for
the rest of your life with him. This is not taking anything
away from Dad, but I would have no problem at all seeing
Dr. Dorster as my Dad. Frankly, I hate calling him Dr.
Dorster."

"OK. So we are really talking about two different things

here. One is whether or not to pick up and move to Mandeville. We can decide that at any time. The other thing is, whether or not I should marry Leit. He sort of 'almost' proposed but not in any formal way. I could take as long as I need to decide on that, but I know that is what Leit wants. So, can I say that you would be OK on doing both – one immediately and the other when and if the time is right?"

"Absolutely, Mom. Yes! Absolutely!"

"Then let's look for the right time to tell Leit and Cassia our thinking about the move. And please hold off on telling the Rodriguiz about that until it is settled with Leit and Cassia. I am not too sure they won't think we are a bit crazy to decide something like this in less than a week. Maybe we are a little crazy too. But I agree with you that it is what we ought to do."

"OK, Mom, I'll race you down the hill!"

"Give me five seconds head start!"

Jacqueline picked up Richard at 11:00 and the 'rest of the quartette' had a light salad lunch and then sat out on their screened back porch. Cassia had some beans she was snapping and so each of the three took a pan of beans and they sat in a semi circle and talked as they snapped.

"Now, does the Training School have 1st through 12th

grades,"asked Gloria.

"Yes," said Leit, "Actually, we have a kindergarten program and then all twelve grades. Then we have the Theology School, the Business School, and the Natural Science School.

"Do you work at the school, Cassia, or what do you do to occupy your time?"
"I have a teaching job at the school. I teach the Third Grade and I love it! Those children are at an age when it is a joy to work with them."

"When does school start in Mandeville," asked Gloria. Leit answered, "Public school begins on September 7th this year and our school begins three days later on the 10th.

The three enjoyed the afternoon, getting to know each other better. Gloria would ask questions and her questions would stir questions that they wanted to ask her. It was a very productive afternoon and it furthered Gloria's assurance that she was doing the right thing.

Richard came back from the picnic just in time to take a bath before supper. At supper time, Cassia asked him if he had a good time.

"Aunt Cassia, honestly, Jacqueline and her family are so much fun to be with. I am really going to miss them. They feel just like family already!"

After supper, everyone was sitting around the living room and Gloria said, "Richard, has Jacqueline said anything about which school she attends?"

"Oh, yes. She is a rising junior and she goes to the West Indian High School."

"Yes," said Leit, she is one of our finest students."

"Did she make any comments about the school itself?"

"Yes. She raves about the school. She says that all of the teachers are very dedicated and well trained."

"Leit," said Gloria, "How do you project the time table for the development of the four year university, say, in terms of Jacqueline's education?"

"Well, of course, anything I say is a rough estimate, but we have already applied for recognition as a Junior College and have met those requirements. That recognition could come through at any time. We should certainly have that in place by the time she graduates from high school in two years. If we get the support that I feel we are going to get for the four year program, thanks to you and Richard, I think the other two years should be in place within the four years before Jacqueline reaches that point. If not, then she and the other students will just do what Melvin, Cassia, and I did. We have an agreement with several senior colleges in Florida that facilitates our students going to those schools."

"Well, since we are in the mode of finding out details about Mandeville, just suppose someone, who was a realtor, wanted to come here to live – now I am not saying that I know such a person, but just supposing – are there several Real Estate Firms here that might need such a realtor?"

Both Leit and Cassia had to hold themselves back from gushing their excitement at the strong possibility that Gloria was suggesting, but then they caught themselves and played along with Gloria's "supposing game".

"Well," said Leit, If such a person were to come, and if such a person wanted to work in such a job, there are three real estate companies here in Mandeville, all with which I am well acquainted, who would fight over the opportunity to have such a person affiliate with them."

"Plus," said Cassia, "There are jobs at the school which would probably fit the interests and talents of such a person."

"In addition to that," added Leit, "The school has been looking for someone with the background to teach 'Music Appreciation' and if this person had as much knowledge of good music as you have recently demonstrated, I am sure the school would feel that they had found the very person they have been seeking."

Gloria almost cried as she tried to continue and she almost stopped, but she was determined to say all that she had planned to say. "Well, so much has been said about our getting Jamaican sand in our shoes and Richard and I have talked together about our feelings about Mandeville and about you two and the other friends that we have met here, and we have decided that we have got to come here to live. We love Mandeville and we both feel that we would just be miserable if we tried to live in London after tasting what life is like in Jamaica. So, what we intend, Leit and Cassia, is to go back to London, place our house on the market with my friends in the real estate office there, ship the things we 'can't do without' here to Mandeville, and rent a house or apartment here until we can sell the house in London. I guess some people would say that we are acting foolishly after just being here for a few days, but we are both strangely very sure that this is the right thing for us to do."

Leit and Cassia both came over and said, "Let's have a group hug!" They all four hugged and then Leit said, "I am sure you know how happy this makes me and Cassia feel. We will do anything to help you in this. Stay with us as long as you need to when you come back."

Cassia added, "I know that there will be many other people here in Mandeville who will also be very happy that you are coming back. If you wish, we will be very happy to help you make some job connections. We are both so happy that we are almost speechless."

Leit thought to himself, "I have practiced my proposal over and over. Should I make it right now on bowed knee or wait until Thursday night or Friday morning? Perhaps I should let well enough alone for now."

Chapter 22. "First Kiss".

It is Wednesday morning. Gloria wakes up with just one thing on her mind. She has been grossly unfair to Thomas Lawn. He had worked tirelessly to help her and Richard, and the thanks that she gave him was to neglect his one request – to keep him informed. She would not fail him today. As soon as breakfast was finished, she asked Leit to please set up a long distance call. She was primed with her mea culpa speech, but his phone rang over and over with no answer. She had missed him. She would call again before lunch. She put aside her sense of guilt, temporarily, and remembered that this was her last full day in Mandeville (hopefully this would be a very short absence).

Leit asked if the three of them could meet him in the living room for a few minutes to go over the schedule for the rest of the week. He read them the article in the paper concerning the meeting that evening at the school. It had run for three mornings, Monday through Wednesday. The article was well written and mentioned that there would be a special meeting in the Chapel of the school at 7:00 P.M. on Wednesday for all students, parents, faculty, and friends of the school, to discuss plans for developing the West Indian Training School into a two year Junior College and then, as soon as possible, into a four year university. It also mentioned that there would be a report and news concerning the disappearance of Dr. Melvin Dorster in March of 1942. Leit said that he thought that the attendance would be very good for that meeting and that they could basically do the same presentation that they had made at the Board of Directors' Meeting on Monday. In addition, he was to have a meeting this morning at 10:00 with the Chairman of the Board of Directors and work out with him what could be said for sure at this stage concerning our goals for a four year university, what would have to be done in stages for the school to qualify, and who would be working on a task force to study and set up the detailed requirements of the project.

"This morning, during my meeting at 10:00, Cassia would like to take both of you with her to visit around the school to meet any faculty or administrative personnel who might be at the school. They could also fill out any preliminary information forms that might make it possible for Gloria to be considered for positions currently open in the school. You could also find out what information Richard needs to bring back from his school in London."

"After lunch the time is free until supper and the meeting at 7:00. The meeting should go on until 8:30 or 9:00, I would think, but could be longer with questions."

If you have any clothes to be washed we can do that this afternoon. Now, tomorrow we are due at Headquarters House, which is the seat of the Legislature, at 2:00, for the meeting with the Education Committee of the Legislature. I know where we are to go but I would like for us to leave here by 10:00. That would put us in Kingston by noon and we can eat lunch at a nice restaurant near the Headquarters

House and then be at our meeting a few minutes early."

Then we could take whatever extra time there is before dinner either to do a little sight seeing or, if we are tired, to go on by the hotel and rest a while. We have reservations at the Courtleigh Hotel and Suites. Now, I know that I have done a lot of talking but the floor is now open for questions or comments."

"I have a comment, Leit. I am very impressed with your thorough planning. I think you have covered everything very well and I do not have any questions at this point. But you have picked up the tab on everything so far and I don't think you should pay the hotel charges for Richard and me. I would feel much better if you will allow us to pay our part."

"Gloria, I would not knowingly cause you discomfort for anything, but in this case you are our guests and we could not possibly allow you to spend any money while you are here. Perhaps, when you come back, we will allow you to buy something with your own money. But not now. I do apologize for being bull headed about that."

"I accept your apology and also appreciate your generosity. Richard and I both thank you."

"OK. The hotel is just a few minutes from the airport where you came in. Since you need to be at the plane a little before 6:00, we can make some arrangements to have breakfast in the suite before we leave. Leaving at 5:00 should give us plenty of time for you to be on the plane before 6:00."

"Now, after our meeting at the school, we can come home for lunch and then the afternoon is open. Does anyone have any ideas about this afternoon?"

"I do have a request, Dr. Dorster. I could not tell the Rodriguiz about our plans to return because we wanted you and Aunt Cassia to be the first to know. So they were a bit sad yesterday about our leaving and I told them that I would try to go back to see them this afternoon. I do believe they will consider this 'good news'."

"I believe you will probably hear them shout for joy at least two blocks away, Richard. So, according to what others might want to do this afternoon, you can either use the Nash or else we can drop you off if we go somewhere. Now, unless somebody has something else, we probably should leave in about 30 minutes – about 9:30, to get to the school a little before 10:00."

At 9:45, the group pulled into the parking lot of the school. Leit met with a very optimistic Board of Directors. They asked Leit if he would be Chairman of a task force to project a timetable and a plan for the development of West Indian Training School into a four year university. The committee was chosen and initial assignments were made. Some were to research the qualifications for a university.

Some were to study the intermediate qualifications for a junior college and how close the school was, currently, to meeting those standards. Others were to look into the costs for building the additional buildings and hiring additional faculty. Lastly, a group was to look into the whole area of endowments, gifts, and financial campaigns. Everyone on the task force was 'fired up and ready to go'.

Cassia introduced Gloria and Richard to several of the faculty members that she saw in the halls, and mentioned that Gloria was planning to move to Mandeville with her son and that he planned to attend the high school. She then took them to several offices, such as the Personnel Office. Mrs. Keenan was in her office. She was the person most responsible for hiring new teachers. Cassia mentioned Gloria's interest in teaching Music Appreciation. Cassia was aware that the two years of college that Gloria had picked up in London was insufficient but felt that the college might allow her to supplement her education during the period when the school was developing its own credentials. Mrs. Keenan agreed to that possibility.

Richard met some of the teachers that he would have as a junior and filled out some preliminary enrollment forms. All in all it was a very productive morning.

When they returned home, Gloria remembered to call Thom. She gave a very thorough report of all the things they had done, especially the groups that they had spoken to and ot their plans for Thursday. There was no way that she would tell him, over the telephone, of her plans to live in Mandeville. She felt better, now that she had done her duty toward Thom.

After lunch it was determined that Gloria had plenty to do to get her and Richard's clothes ready for the trip, so Richard took the Nash and Leit went into his study to prepare a few extra thoughts for his evening presentation. Since he was now Chairman, basically, of the whole campaign, the success or failure of the campaign would largely rest on his shoulders.

Gloria checked with Cassia about the use of the washer and dryer and processed the dirty clothes. A bit of ironing was also needed. Cassia busied herself with supper preparation. On several occasions during the afternoon, she came by and commented on how glad she was that Gloria was coming back. The last time she said, "I am so happy to finally have a sister, after all these years!"

When Leit heard all of the noise in the laundry room subside, he checked with Gloria to see how much more work she had to do. She told him that she had about three pieces to iron and that she should be through in about twenty minutes. He asked if she would like to take a walk and she said that she would really like to see the view from the top of the hill again. So Leit said, "It's a date! Thirty minutes!"

Leit came back to the kitchen and let Cassia know where

they would be. She said that they would be ready to eat in about forty five minutes.

As they walked up the hill, Gloria said, "Did you have many kids in your neighborhood when you were growing up?"

"Yes. Lots of kids. We were free to roam within a range of about ten blocks in each direction from the house, as long as we let my folks know where we were going. It was usually to one of three different friend's houses. Each friend had other kids in his neighborhood that we got to know. Most of the kids we knew at school."

"Did you play games like, 'Red light' and 'Mother May I'?"

"Yes, we knew those games. We also played soccer and several types of 'Run and Tag' games."

At the top of the hill they sat down. "What is your favorite color, Leit?"

"Yellow, for sure. How about yours?"
"It is a toss up between red and yellow. I really could not pick one over the other. How about your favorite music?"

"Well, I love classical, as you know – of that I favor Rachmaninoff and Elgar, also Grieg. But I also like certain of the Jamaican Mento numbers. I think you will like it too when you hear more of it. OK. It's my turn to ask you. I seem to have something about me that attracts you and I thank Heaven for that. But I am more than a little curious as to what that is. I know that I am being very vain but somehow I feel comfortable about asking you."

"Hmm...I should be able to answer that easily. The last thing I do every night before I go to sleep is picture your face. I really like your gray, wavy hair. I like your face that smiles so very easily. I like your kind eyes. I like your consideration for others – not just of me, for you might just be trying to impress me. No, you are considerate of the boy that you buy your newspaper from. I like the love and respect that you show for your sister. I love your openness – your transparency. I love that you have classical records that are not just for 'show' – you actually listen to them and appreciate them. I love that God has somehow chosen you to be the one to show me that I have more to look forward to in life than just seeing my wonderful son grow up and be a man, as terrific as that is. Now, I think that I have said enough! In fact I think I overdid it! Now, you owe me!"

"I can't do it half as well as you just did it for me, Gloria. But I will give it a try. I've got to start with your laugh. Your wonderful laugh lifts me up! It affirms me. It says, 'You truly are someone special'. It even sometimes says, 'I love you very much!' I don't know if you knew all of that about your laugh. I love everything about your beautiful face. I love the way you bite your bottom lip when you are thinking hard. I love that tears come in your eyes when you listen to Rachmaninoff and when you talk to little girls who beg you to stay in Mandeville. I love that you like to be on this hill, which is my favorite spot on earth. And I can't say it any more beautifully than you have just said it - ' I love that God has chosen you to show me that I have more to look forward to than just being a father to the young people who grow up in my classes and then leave to give themselves to life."

"Gloria, you said you would not want to hear my proposal until I was ready and until I was able to present the best and most well thought out proposal that I am capable of. I think I am ready for that, and...."

"Oh, Leit. I think I am as anxious to hear it as you are to speak it. But somehow I don't want Richard and Cassia to just hear about it later. I want them to hear it when you do it. Would you mind very much if we wait until just the right time when they are with us?"

"I will wait on one condition. Do you realize that we have reached this point where I am ready to propose marriage, and we have never kissed? Wouldn't it be awful if you married me and then found out that I am just a terrible kisser?"

"I think if that were to happen I would feel like getting our marriage annulled, Leit. There fore, I demand that you not wait another second. I want you to kiss me RIGHT NOW!"

Leit put his arm around Gloria and bent over to give his

best Clark Gable kiss, but at that point he thought of how cute she had been when she said, 'kiss me RIGHT NOW!' and he started to giggle. He couldn't stop. Gloria caught the giggles then, and every time he started to kiss her they both began to giggle again. They finally gave up and just hugged each other, full of the joy of being in each other's life.

They realized that it was time to be at supper, so they ran down the hill holding hands. When they came around the house to the front door, Leit took her in his arms and gave her a real Clark Gable / Vivian Leigh kiss.

"Oh, My goodness! Oh Leit! Believe me, that will do JUST FINE!"

They had not noticed that Richard had just pulled up in the Nash. He got out and was grinning from ear to ear as he came up the walk way.
"You saw, didn't you?" laughed Gloria.
"I'll never tell!" laughed Richard.
Leit thought to himself, "Perhaps someone else also got a first kiss!"

Chapter 23. "Sweet and Sour".

For dinner on Wednesday evening, Cassia had prepared a very elegant Jamaican meal. When Richard and Gloria sat down and Cassia began to bring in the bowls, Gloria said, "Now I understand why You busied yourself all afternoon in the kitchen, Cassia. This is really special!"

"I wanted it to be special on your last night (for a while) with us."

Richard said, "OK, now tell us what each thing on the table is called."

"Well, we start with a red pea bisque with rum flambe. Then, over here is the main dish – a quava stuffed chicken with caramelized mango. This is a sauteed chayote with garlic and herbs. Chayote is sort of a gourd – like fruit that grows on a vine. You can decide whether you like it or not. Then this is sweet potato, onion, and apple gratin. Later on I will bring out the dessert, which is rum cake with rum raisin ice cream and island fruit.

Leit asked the blessing and thanked God not only for the food but for the gift of the new friendships that had been formed this week.

Everyone ate more than usual and began to say that they would do well to get through the evening without falling asleep prematurely. Richard was delirious over the dessert, which he had never tasted before.

Reluctantly they got up and prepared to go to the school. They got there just five minutes until 7:00, and went up on the stage with the chairman of the Board of Directors and several of the School Administrators.

The Chairman of the Board of Directors got up and said, very briefly, "I appreciate your presence here tonight. You will know very shortly why we invited you here. I believe that you will be very glad that you came. I am happy to present Richard Parsons and his mother, Mrs. Gloria Parsons – both of London, and someone that you know very well, Dr. Leitman Dorster.

There was moderate applause from the audience, most of which had very little idea why they had been invited to come. Richard rose from his chair and went to the podium. After a pause for composure, he began. "Thank you for welcoming us so generously. I am just an average guy from London, a rising Junior in high school, whom God allowed to have a part in a miracle. This simple glass bottle was another part of that miracle." Then he told the simple story that you read in the first chapter. When he got to the message itself, there was not a sound to be heard in that large auditorium. Richard's eyes were so full that he could hardly read. The same was true of the whole audience.

Then his mother rose and joined Richard. He moved to the right so that she could approach the microphone.

She picked up the story at the point where they decided to do all they could to find any friends or loved ones of those three men named in the message. She told how they had found Clara Woosley, the one who was to have married Jim Stark the next time he came home. Then she told how they had found the connection with the West Indian Training School and how Sir Thomas Lawn had arranged their trip to Jamaica and how the key message had come over the airplane radio just before they reached Jamaica. She read the part of the speech that Clara had retrieved from her letter from Jim. When she read the part that said, "With God's help and the help of my fellow country men, it WILL happen!" she became silent. But all over the auditorium was heard the word, "yes", "yes", and "yes!"

Then Leit stepped up as Richard stayed on his right and Gloria moved to his left. Since Leit's part would be a little longer than usual, Richard and Gloria returned to their seats.

Leit did a very fine job of presenting a challenge to the group that would not be easy but was well within the ability of the school, with the help of Mandeville and all of Jamaica, to accomplish. Gloria and Richard were both very proud of Leit as he shown like a diamond in the bright light of destiny.

When the time for questions came, the usual questions

came that they had heard several times before and had anticipated. But then one question came for Richard from a young lady about his same age. She said, "Richard, has finding the message had any lasting effects on you? And, if 'yes', how? And has the experience of these three men made you afraid to be on the sea again?"

Richard was stunned by the question and, for a moment, was silent. Then he said, "What a wonderful question. We have been before several groups since we came here last Wednesday but this is the first time that this question has been asked. I would like very much to answer it as truthfully as possible and I would like to address your last question first. "Has it made me afraid to be on the sea again?" We came to Mandeville almost immediately after finding the message. While here I have been on the open sea in Dr. Dorster's sail boat and I was on a lake in a much smaller boat. In neither instance did I experience any fear. I also flew over a vast expanse of ocean in order to get here and the only fear I felt was my inexperience in flying itself. But, and this is the first time that I have thought of this, on both occasions in boats I automatically thought of those men and the sacrifice that they made. It would be my guess that any time I find myself over a body of water, whether on boat or an airplane, I will be given the gift of remembering those men.

"As to the effects of the message on my life, the first effect has been that I placed all of my private interests on hold in order that my mother and I could do all we needed to do to carry this message to any person that can benefit by it. We are still on that mission. Secondly, I seem to have been given a great deal of added maturity, which I count as an outright gift that I did nothing to earn. I find that I have a greater respect for life and its vulnerability and its great value. I have a greater desire to be the very best person that I am capable of being. After hearing the speech that Dr. Melvin Dorster was allowed to deliver only to us, I have a greater desire to get as fine an education as I can. Thank you for that question. It did me a great deal of good to put that into words!"

The rest of the evening was much like the other two events – the concert and the Festival in Christiana. There was a standing ovation that lasted at least five minutes. Richard was especially pleased to see that the Rodriguez had come. Jacqueline just beamed her admiration for Richard. When she was ready to leave she unobtrusively reached for his hand and left a small folded note in his palm. When he was able to get by himself for a moment he read it's message – "I will be counting the days until I can be with you again. Jackie."

On the way home they discussed the program and everyone was pleased with the over all response. Gloria, Richard, and Cassia expressed how proud they were of Leit's presentation. "Thank you", responded Leit. "It occurred to me that we have refined our presentation so well that, when Gloria and Richard return, we ought to "Go on the road" on the week ends and present this all over Jamaica to any group that would allow us. It would also be a way for you two to see much of Jamaica."

"I would be available for that, school work allowing!" replied Richard.

"Me too!" said Gloria.

"I'll stay back and cook", laughed Cassia.

When they got home, Cassia said that there was some rum cake with raisin ice cream left for anyone interested. No one could resist.

The next morning, after breakfast, Gloria packed the two suit cases and relaxed in the living room. Everyone had bathed and dressed for the day before breakfast. Richard was making one more phone call to Jackie. Cassia was putting away the dishes.

Leit had put on Debussy's "Prelude to the Afternoon of a Faun" on the player. "You seem to know just what to play and when to play it, Leit," commented Gloria.

"Would you like to have one more look at the top of the hill when this is over?" asked Leit.

"Oh, Yes!" answered Gloria.

They walked up the hill at a brisk pace, holding hands. At

the top they stood and inhaled the fresh morning air. "It is almost as if the sea were right here next to us, yet it is miles away," mused Gloria.

"But remember, it is all around us on every side. It is as though we were still safe in the womb of God, here cn our island. It is your island too, My Dear Gloria! Just wait until you stand in this spot at night. You will be absolutely transported."

"It's a date, Leit – the very first night that we are back, after supper, this very spot!"

Leit gave a very long and convincing impersonation of Clark Gable. This time with no giggles at all.

At 10:00, everyone was ready and they headed toward Kingston. Gloria and Richard noticed things they remembered from their previous trip down this highway. Leit pointed out industrial sites, farms, sugar cane plantations, and other interesting attractions. At approximately 12:00 they pulled into Hinely's Restaurant. "This is a very nice restaurant", said Leit, "and they have a good variety of food." Everyone was very pleased with their lunch. Each person ate lightly because they did not want to be overly full when they made their presentation. It was now 1:15, so they road around the Government area for a few minutes while Leit pointed out the different buildings of significance. When they got to Orange St. they drove until they turned on Beeston, and as they got to

Duke St. Leit turned the corner and Gloria and Richard
saw this beautiful building that looked more like a majestic
private home than a Government building. Leit said, "This
is it – Headquarters House – the seat of our Legislature."

Leit parked the car and went into the main entrance. They
were met by two gentlemen who asked if they could be of
service. Leit gave their names and said that they were to
meet with the Education Committee. One of the gentlemen
said, "Yes, they are expecting you. They will be
assembling in Conference Room 205 in about ten minutes.
You may go there now if you wish. You should ask for
Senator Joseph Homes. He will be hosting the meeting
today."

When they found the room and walked inside, Senator
Homes was waiting for them. He introduced himself and
Leit did the introductions of his group. Senator Homes
took them to the dais where their chairs were already
arranged behind a podium. The other Committee members
began to come in and take their places at individual desks
arranged in a semi circle in front of the podium. There
were about 35 members on the Committee and all were
present.

Senator Homes said, "Gentlemen, I have called this
meeting today because the nature of our visitors' business
is certainly paramount to our interests in the Higher
Education of Jamaica's young men and women. You are all
aware of the wonderful history of the West Indian Training

School. Now the School is on the threshold of launching the bid for full university recognition. I know that you will want to hear the interesting story that has led to this decision. I would like to introduce Dr. Leitman Dorster, the Head of the School of Theology at West Indian Training School. He will introduce the others."
 Cassia was privileged to sit with the group on the dais and was introduced, though she did not speak.

The rest of the presentation was almost a duplication of what had been done in the meeting at the school the night before. Questions concerning the plans for qualifying for four year accreditation were the primary interest of the Senators. But one Senator stood and said, "If I recall correctly from what Mrs. Parsons said, you still have no clue concerning the location of the family and friends of a Bob Swithers. I might just have something that will be helpful to you. There was a Fire Chiefs' Convention here in Kingston about ten years ago. One of the main speakers was the Fire Chief of Leeds and his name was Robert Swithers. I remembered the name because it was so unusual. Mr. Swithers mentioned in his address that he had a son in the Royal Navy that was lost at sea and that it was much more difficult to lose someone that you love if you have no idea at all what happened to them. I think that could very well be the chap that you are looking for. '

Gloria, Richard, and Leit were ecstatic. They could not thank the Senator enough for his help. When the meeting was over, the response had been all that Leit had hoped for and more. "What a sweet and wonderful day this has turned out to be," thought Gloria.

They went to the car as happy as larks. It was only 3:30, but they decided to go to their hotel and rest for a while before supper, rather than do any more sight seeing. Gloria noticed that Cassia had been quieter than usual and asked if she felt OK. Cassia said, "I do feel a little warm as though I might have a little fever. I am sure it is nothing but a change of schedule this week."

Gloria felt her head and said, "Cassia, you do have a little fever. Do you have any other symptoms?"

"Well, I have sort of a 'flu – like' feeling all over."

"Perhaps we should take you by a physician just to check you out."

"Oh, I will be all right I am sure. We can get some aspirin at the hotel and that should take care of it!"

They pulled up to the beautiful, old Courtleigh Hotel and Suites on Knutsford Boulevard and parked near the baggage entrance. A porter tended to their baggage and they checked in at the desk. They were given Suite 518. Leit asked where he could purchase some aspirin and was directed to the Magazine and Gift Shop in the Lobby. When they got to the room, Cassia took two aspirin and laid down on the bed. Everyone was a little uneasy and

Leit and Gloria went into the adjoining room to discuss what they should do. Leit decided to go back to the desk and ask the best procedure for getting routine medical help. They told him that there was a hospital just a few blocks away with a very good emergency clinic that would take care of their needs safely and efficiently. She gave them a diagram of how to get from the Hotel to the Emergency Entrance.

Leit went back to the room and told Cassia what they had found out. He suggested that they go over there immediately. Cassia said, "Oh, I hate that this has happened with Gloria and Richard here. I am ordinarily as healthy as a horse! Let's give the aspirin a little longer."

At 5:00 Gloria felt of Cassia's head. "You do not feel any better do you, Cassia? Because I believe you still have fever."

"I am afraid you are right, Gloria. I am so sorry about this. But I guess we had better go see what this is all about." They suggested that Richard stay and rest but he wanted to go with "Aunt Cassia".

So, everyone got in the Nash and went to the Emergency Room. The nurse checked her vital signs and took a routine urine sample. In a few minutes a doctor came out. "The good news is that this is not serious. It is a common urinary infection that is easily treatable and lasts just two or three days when treated. The bad news is that you are going to feel symptoms similar to the flu for a couple of days. I am going to give you a powerful antibiotic that will make you sleep for about 12 hours. Then you should take the tablets I will give you as directed until all of them are gone. Don't stop just because you feel better. Take all of them. Are you allergic to any medicine that you know of?" Cassia nodded her head "No".

This first medicine should "get this bug on the run". But you should go home and go to bed. You probably won't feel like eating any supper. Just rest and I would suggest you stay in bed until probably 10:00 in the morning. After that you can do anything you feel like doing. OK? I can just about guarantee that you will feel much better tomorrow."

They all thanked the doctor, paid a modest fee, and went back to their rooms. "I am so sorry, Gloria. I'm messing up everything!"

"No you are not! The only thing you are going to miss is seeing us off on the plane. You definitely need to sleep late tomorrow. You don't need to be getting up at 4:00 in the morning."

"Yes, Nurse Gloria! Actually, he wasn't kidding about that being a powerful medicine he gave me. I feel as though I had better give you a good bye kiss (I'm not contagious) and a hug right now. I feel like I am going to 'sleepy, sleepy land' in about 5 seconds."

"Good, that is what you need. So, give us each a hug and we thank you for all the sweet things that you have done for us this week. We promise that we will be back in Mandeville just as soon as possible. We will keep you informed by telephone."

Leit went with Gloria into the other suite. Richard decided to lie down for a few minutes. They decided to wait a few minutes and then order a light supper with room service and go to bed early.

As Leit and Gloria sat on the sofa, they snuggled a bit and he said, "Well, Dear Gloria. I had my proposal all geared up and ready to go, but we do want a healthy audience for that performance. So, will you mind waiting until your return to Mandeville?"

"My Darling Leit. You have already made a permanent commitment from your heart to my heart. The words are just a formality – an important formality to be sure, but you are already caught – hook, line, and sinker. So I do not mind waiting a few more days. I am sure you know what the answer will be when you do get to "give your performance". Right now I will settle for your rendition of "Gable and Leigh"!

Chapter 24. "Mayday, Mayday, Mayday".

On Friday morning, Gloria had a wake up call in her suite so that it would not bother Cassia. Then she came in and touched Leit quietly to wake him. She had ordered a light breakfast for the three of them to be delivered at 4:30. She took her shower quickly and then Richard took his. By 4:30, everyone was dressed and ready to go as soon as breakfast was finished.Gloria went in and felt of Cassia's head. It now felt normal. The breakfast arrived promptly at 4:30.

Leit said that Cassia had slept soundly as expected. He felt that she would be safe if he were gone just a little over an hour. He did leave a note on his bed in case she should wake up and forget where he had gone.

They left just a few minutes after 5:00. They arrived at the airport at 5:40 and Gloria and Richard filled out a brief form. Leit got on the plane and Gloria introduced him to Henry, Jeff, Peter, and Riley. Since the plane was just warming up and there was a little time to spare, Gloria asked Riley, who was from Leeds, if he knew anyone in Leeds by the name of Swithers. He answered, "Mrs. Parsons, you know, when you told us the story of the Message, it did not ring a bell that you could be talking about one of our guys. But, there are several families of Swithers, all related, in Leeds. I just never knew a Bob. Of course, I would have been only 10 years old when he disappeared. After you left I remembered that our Fire

Chief, James Swithers, had a son that was lost in the war. I guess there is a good chance that he was your Bob Swithers."

"Thank you, Riley. That confirms what a gentleman here in Kingston said. He had met a James Swithers from Leeds at a Fire Chiefs' Convention, and that gentleman too, had lost a son in the war. So it looks very much as though the end might be in sight for our quest.

They placed the suit cases in the storage area and Richard took his seat after saying "Good Bye" to Leit. Gloria went back out with Leit and they said their farewells in private.

Gloria got into her seat. Then Henry came back and said, "Now, let's go over the details of our safety procedures again because we have to take this very seriously when we fly over this much ocean." Then he went over the procedure for putting on the inflatable vests. He showed them where the inflatable life rafts were stored and how to inflate them. Lastly he sat in a seat across the aisle and demonstrated how to bend over and place your head if the plane had to land on the water.

Richard said, "This is a different plane than the one we came on, I believe. The other had 4 engines and this has 2."

"Yes," answered Henry, they are giving the DC4 an overhaul, so they are using this DC3 this week. It just has

2 engines but they are very dependable planes, so don't worry.

Richard noticed that some of the paint and the seat upholstery was showing considerable wear, so he did worry just a little. When Henry went back to the cockpit, Richard said to Gloria, "I was just thinking about that girl's question on Wednesday evening, about whether I had more fear of the ocean because of the message. You know, I really don't. I'm even getting a little more used to airplanes. But when I was in Dr. Dorster's boat I felt totally free!"

"So did I, Richard. So did I." The reference to the sail boat trip brought back memories that Gloria could "bask" in for a good long while as she recalled the feel of the breeze, the smell of the ocean, and the first real time she had had alone with Leit. She could not help but smile as she thought of their future together.

Richard and Gloria both had books to read and that kept them occupied until they landed in Nassau for refueling. She went into the cockpit once to ask Riley about how far Leeds is from London. He said that it would be about 270 kilometers so allow about 3 to 3 ½ hours one way. She came back and reported that to Richard.

After they left Nassau they read some more. Finally, after several hours, Gloria said, "Richard, I am as anxious to get back to Mandeville as you are. How do you feel about this, and I have no preference one way or the other. Do you think we should take off to Leeds on Saturday to finalize that one last piece to our puzzle, and then come back to London on Sunday if possible? Or do you think that I should go and talk with my Boss tomorrow about leaving London and go ahead and list the house to sell immediately? Should we sell it furnished or ship our furniture to Mandeville? Should we ship the car to Mandeville or sell it here and buy another one there?"

"Woa, Mom! You just unloaded a bunch of stuff there!"

"Well, as far as I can see, that is about every decision that we will need to make before we leave for Mandeville. You are the man of the house and I trust your judgment. Oh, and should we fly or go by ship?"

"OK, you know how my mind works. Let me get my notebook out and write out each of these questions so that I can sit here and ponder for a while. Then I will let you know what I think about each one. Now, help me remember: Go to Leeds first or go to your Boss to resign and list the house first. List the house furnished or ship the furniture to Mandeville. Should we ship the car to Mandeville or sell it here and buy another one there. Should we go back on ship or plane. Let me sit here a few minutes and think about this."

At about 1:30 the plane banked for the landing approach at Bermuda. Everyone got off the plane as it was being refueled and they met the other flight crew. They all had lunch at an airport restaurant and then the other flllight crew took over for the flight on in to London.

After about 30 minutes of looking at his list, Richard was ready with some tentative thoughts about the questions that Gloria had asked him earlier. "Now, all of this is just my first impression, so don't write any of it in stone."

1. I am anxious to resolve the Bob Swithers question. But I think we can do a better job with that if we get some of this other business off of our minds. So, I think , go over to your Boss the first thing tomorrow. Tell him we fell in love with Jamaica and that is where we are going to live – crazy or not. (You don't have to tell him that you fell head over heels in love with a super guy!)."

"You devil!" teased Gloria.

"Well, I am your son! What can I say!"

2. So, I would say, sell the furniture with the house. Most of it is 15 or 20 years old. Except for one or two little items, I don't have any sentimental attachments. If you do then we can ship what you want to keep.

3. If I stay home while you go to see your Boss, I can call some places about the cost of shipping the car. It sort of boils down to the cost of shipping balanced against the cost of a new car.

4. Then, if you get squared away by early afternoon we could run on over to Leeds and maybe even work in a visit in the evening. At least we would be ready to do something on Sunday. Then we could come back Sunday evening or Monday morning.

5. Then about how we go back. I guess we need to find out how the cost of air fare compares with the price of the ship ticket. Also, is taking the extra time to get there worth the amount we might save?

Gloria said, "All of that makes good sense! Let's go with it just like you said.. OK, I think I will read until we get to the refueling in Ponta Delgada and I think I will run into the coffee shop there and get me some coffee and a big sweet roll. How about you?"
"That sounds good to me. Let's see, It's almost 5:00 now, so I think I will take a short snooze."
Gloria decided, "I think I'll just read a little..."

There was a "popping " sound in the right engine and it made Richard a little concerned. He looked out the window and saw some smoke billowing out of the engine. He got up from his seat and went into the cockpit. He looked toward the navigators and both were looking out at the smoke. "Are we OK?" said Richard to whomever would answer.

"Don't worry, Richard," said the copilot. "This plane can fly all day on one engine if it became necessary!"

The copilot indicated to the pilot that he had turned off and secured the right engine. "We need to see if we can gain a little altitude, Sir."

"I'm 'goosing ' it, Jeff, but it isn't responding."

Richard thought he heard a little more concern in the pilot's voice than before.

"We are losing altitude, Sir!" advised Jeff.

"Peter, get Ponta Delgada and give a 'Mayday'!" said Henry.

Peter tuned into the emergency frequency and shouted, "Mayday, Mayday, Mayday". (Mayday is the international call for help and goes out to all ships and planes that have their radios on. It is always shouted three times so that there is no question about what is being conveyed). Peter gave his coordinates of longitude and latitude and then switched to the Ponta Delgada frequency . "Ponta Delgada, this is DC3 – XC – NI30Q . We have lost our right engine and are losing altitude. We have ten souls aboard and the information on crew and passengers was filed in Kingston and Bermuda. We have probably less than ten minutes ET until ditch." He then gave the coordinates.

Riley came into the passenger compartment and said, "The one engine doesn't seem to be able to maintain our altitude, folks. Unless that improves, it looks like we are going to have to ditch. These planes do that very well. Please put on your flotation vests but do not pull your inflation lanyard until we say to. I am going to get out three of the inflatable life rafts, just in case. Do you remember how to put your head down? Let me see how you do it. Yep, that's good. Both of you are doing it right. Keep buckled up, please. We will keep you informed."

In the cockpit, Henry said, "I have been working with the throttle and the fuel mixture and nothing seems to help. I think we will be in the drink within five minutes. Relay that to Ponta Delgada, Peter – five minutes ET until ditch."

Peter said, "Henry, they responded affirmatively to my location coordinates but now I am getting no response at all. Looks like the radio is out."

"Jeff, check the electrical circuits", said Henry.

"Everything seems to be out, Henry."

"OK. Two minutes until ditch. Riley, check the passengers. Tell them to inflate their vests as soon as we come to
a stop. Be ready to inflate the three rafts. Get out a fourth for back up. Thirty seconds until ditch. Everyone buckle your seat belts. It might be a good idea to say a prayer."

There was a "swoosh" sound and then a continuous

bouncing motion for about thirty seconds, then nothing but quiet.

"Sound off if you are OK!" said Henry.

"Gloria, OK!"

"Richard, OK!"

Everyone in the cockpit was fine.

Henry yelled, "OK, we have several minutes so don't panic. Riley and Peter will open the door and inflate the rafts. Try to get in the rafts without falling in the water. You will be more comfortable later if you don't get soaked now. Three of us in each raft. Riley and Peter, get in with Richard and Gloria. As soon as we are in the water get your paddle and paddle away from the plane because it might create some suction as it goes down. Then take the rope on your rafts and tie the three rafts together. The water is calm, so we are going to be fine!"

When everyone was safely in their raft and away from the plane, Henry said, "Our location is known to Ponta Delgada and probably a half dozen ships in the area from our Mayday. They have at least one operational PBY Catalina flying boat that stays on 'ready' in Ponta Delgada. The Coast Guard has rescue vessels. This is a major shipping lane. Our 'Mayday' went out to everybody near here. So all we need to do is sit tight. If a plane comes by

we will send up a flare. We will put a dye marker on the
water. Whoever picks us up will take us to the nearest
Island and eventually we will get to Ponta Delgada
and either go to London on a commercial flight or the
Navy will send another plane for us. This is inconvenient, I
know, and I am so sorry it happened. But I am so glad that
everyone is safe and sound."

What Henry did not know, was that the PBY Catalina
stationed at Ponta Delgada, was out on another rescue
mission of a sailing vessel that had capsized. It would not
be back to its base for several hours. All the boats in the
area were also hours away from their location.
Richard, who tends to see some humor in everything, said,
"Well, the good thing is, we don't have to worry about
what to do tomorrow!" Gloria looked at Richard and said,
"For a few moments I was afraid that all of that happiness
I have been anticipating was going 'down the drain'. But
you know what? I believe when something like this
happens it always seems to bring some good with it, if you
just take the time to look for it."

"I feel the same way, Mom. Riley, you guys did a great job
of ditching! My compliments!"

"All in a day's work, Richard. We do a lot of training for
this eventuality, because no airplane ever built is 100% all
of the time."

The news was on the radio and television that a Royal

Navy plane, flying from Kingston to London, was down in the ocean out from the Azores. The word was not out yet that their rafts had been located. Leit heard the news and immediately called Sir Thomas. Though he had never spoken to him personally he knew the number. Sir Thomas knew who he was from speaking with Gloria and responded warmly.

Sir Thomas had already received word through the Navy. He said, "I know that you are concerned, Dr. Dorster, and I am too. Let me say that ditching at sea is fairly common and relatively safe. All of our military pilots are well trained for that. I am sure they had life vests and life rafts and that sort of thing. I am in a good position here to be in the "news loop".Let me suggest two possibilities. I will be glad to call you with any news that I receive. Or, if you should desire to fly here to London, if you will call me about when your flight will arrive here, I will be glad to pick you up at the airport and take you wherever you wish to go. Or, I will be glad to have you in my home. Gloria and Richard are friends of mine and friends of yours. To my way of thinking, that makes us friends. So let me know your choice when you have made it."

"Thank you, Sir Thomas. Gloria said that you were a tremendous source of help to her and Richard. I can see that it is true."

It was then 6:00 P.M. Leit called the commercial airport. There was a jet leaving for London at 7:30 P.M. and it would arrive in London at 6:30 in the morning at Croydon Airport in London. He told Cassia that he felt that he should fly to London and wait for Gloria and Richard there. Cassia said, "I feel good enough to go and I'm going with you. See if you can still get two seats and I will go pack a small satchel."

Leit called back and they did have two seats left. He called Sir Thomas and told him their arrival time at Croydon. "Fine. I will pick you both up and you will be my guests for a good London Breakfast. By the way, I just got word that three rafts were spotted and there were definitely ten persons aboard" Leit thanked Sir Thomas. They jumped in the Nash, each with one change of clothes. The plane was already warming up as they purchased their tickets. Fortunately, a light dinner would be served aboard this flight. They wondered if they might be flying close to where Richard and Gloria went down. They were hoping that they could be picked up before dark.

In the three life rafts, everyone was hoping the same thing – that they would be picked up before dark. One plane had spotted them and "wagged" its wings in recognition. But that was an hour ago and nothing since. It was beginning to get dark, and Henry kept looking at an ominous cloud that was forming to the southeast. He did not say anything but Richard did not miss the look of concern on his face.

Jeff suggested that they break open the food packet and have a snack to hold them over. He took out several items and gave Richard and Gloria some of each. Among the items was a small bottle of water. It was no longer closed with a cork, but the resemblance to another bottle was so very close that Richard was stunned at the strange series of events that had placed him and his mother in a little rubber life boat, bobbing on the ocean, with a small glass bottle in their hands. Perhaps, as his mother had said, "When something like this happens, it always brings some good with it if you just take the time to look for it." But it was becoming much darker now, and the cloud was darker still!

Chapter 25. "A Royal Welcome".

As the hint of darkness settled over the vast ocean, the anxiety of the group was toned down a little by the appearance of one of the most beautiful sunsets that anyone in the group had ever seen. No one spoke for a few minutes as they gazed in awe at the majestic sweep across the whole horizon. Peter, who had a nice tenor voice, began to sing,

"Land of Hope and Glory,

Mother of the free,

How shall we extol thee,

Who are born of thee?

Wider still and wider

Shall thy bounds be set,

God, Who made thee mighty,

Make thee mightier yet

God, Who made thee mighty,

Make thee mightier yet!"

By the beginning of the second line, everyone was singing with full voice. They enjoyed it so much that they sang it again. It was as though Gloria could hear the base viols and the tympani drums of the London Symphony playing in the background. When the song finally subsided, everyone in the group had tears on their cheeks.

Richard leaned over to Gloria and said, "Does singing this song give you second thoughts about our moving, Mom?"

"Oh, No. Dear. I will always love England. There is no denying that. But I have room in my heart for England and Jamaica. How about you? What are you feeling?"

"About the same as you. No, I definitely want to go back. I am sure that it will take a while before I have quite the emotional attachment to whatever is Jamaica's national anthem that I have for 'Land of Hope and Glory'. But, like you say, it doesn't have to be one or the other. After all, Jamaica honors our Queen too."

By that time, the sunset had gone entirely. Henry said, "If you haven't located your torch light yet, please do so. Keep it handy because, if you need it you need to have it quickly. I have my torch if you need it to find yours."

Both of the other rafts reported that they had their torches in hand.

"OK. Just one other word about our situation. For some

reason, that I 'm sure we will learn later, the Ponta Delgada PBY flying boat was not available. There is no reason to be overly concerned. I would have preferred to be picked up in the daylight, it is true. But, on the other hand, we can easily spot a ship within miles of here at night. We have a flare gun and flares that a ship can see miles away at night. I really can not see us being out here all night. With as much air and shipping traffic as we will have in these lanes. So just try to rest and know that we are safe. The cloud that came up earlier went somewhere else, so the weather is on our side."

This little pep talk made Gloria and Richard feel much better. Gloria turned to Riley and said, "I don't know if I mentioned it or not, but Richard and I will probably be going to your home town in a few days, to see if we can meet Mrs. Swithers. Do you know if the several Swithers families are closely related?"

"Yes Ma'am, I think that Mr. Swithers, the former Fire Chief, had several children who live in the area. The others are all first cousins."
"Well, what is Leeds like, Riley?" asked Richard.
"It's actually a pretty large city, Richard. It is sort of a cultural, business, and financial center second only to London. It has a very fine university, the University of Leeds. It has a very old history – all the way back to the fifth century. It has grown from being a compact little market town in the sixteenth century, to being a very populous, urban center at the present time. It did that by

absorbing all of the little villages that clustered around it."
"When you do go, I would not be at all surprised if Mr.
Smithers heard your story and said, 'Hey, wait a minute, I
want my whole family to hear this. I want to have a picnic
and let everybody hear it at the same time!"

"Well, Riley, before we came to THIS little picnic, we had
planned to go over to Leeds either tomorrow or Sunday.
But I guess this little delay will change our plans just a
little."

"Lights Ho!" Yelled Henry. "Looks to me like a cruise
ship to starboard. I have the flare gun ready and I am going
to be sparing with these, because I have four flares and
hopefully, you each have four more. But we don't want to
waste them. If they see ours, they should fire one in
recognition. If they don't fire one within a minute or two, I
will fire another."

Everyone strained their eyes, but no flare was seen. .
Henry fired a second flare. There was another period of
waiting. All of a sudden, two flares went up from the other
ship. One flare and then another 30 seconds later.
"That's the most beautiful fireworks display I've seen in
my whole life," said Gloria.

"I am going to fire another series of two, so they can be
sure of our direction. Then we will turn on our torch lights
to give them a constant guidance to us."

Henry fired two more flares and the ship answered with two more.

"Which of you guys are the best at sending and receiving Morse code by light?"

Peter said, "I guess that would be me, Sir. I sort of got interested in morse code in Navigator school and really worked hard on it. So, I think I can read pretty well and, if they can see our torch light, I can send with that. So, we will wait and see what they do. I will start sending 'Please identify yourself' and see if they respond to that."

"Does anyone sense that they are coming this way yet?"asked Henry.

"I definitely think they look bigger than they did a few minutes ago," said Gloria.

"Does anyone have anything to write a message on if I get one?"

"I have a little piece of paper and a pencil in my pocket," said Richard.

"Let somebody hold the light for you and be ready to take down the letters as they come, if they come."

"Here it comes. I D T O F O L L O W. I. D. to follow. Here's more. ..W E A R E Q U E E N OF BERMUDA F U

R N E S S B E R M U D A C R U I S E L I N E E T A Y
O U T E N M I N U T E S W I L L L O W E R S M A L L
B O A T F R O M O U R P O R T S I D E. Read that back,
Richard."

"I D to follow. We are Queen of Bermuda - Furness
Bermuda Cruise Line. E.T. A. (Estimated time of arrival)
you, ten minutes. Will lower small boat from our Port
side."

Peter sent back, "We are nine men, one woman, all
healthy."

"OK, everybody. When they get here, Gloria first, then
Richard. Take your time and watch your step. It would be
a shame to get soaking wet at this stage. We will help you
transfer from the raft to their boat," said Henry.
As the big ship got closer, it turned to starboard to expose
it's port side, then came to an abrupt stop. Those in the
rafts could see a small boat being lowered. What sounded
like hundreds of people were cheering on the deck. When
the small boat touched the water an announcement was
heard on their P.A. System, and the cheering stopped
immediately, probably to aid the rescue operations. The
small powered launch followed the torch lights directly to
the rafts.

The transfer was without incident. Gloria was careful to
protect the brief case that she had kept with her with the
papers, notes, and original message inside. In less than an

hour, the launch was again hooked to its lifters and the whole group was being lifted to the main deck.

When the people on deck saw Gloria step out of the boat they began to cheer again. Gloria was amazed at the finery. All of the women were in elegant gowns and diamond jewelry. The men were either in tuxedo or dinner jacket. A band was playing in the distance.

The Captain greeted them. "I am Captain Cornelius Ferrel and on behalf of The Furness Bermuda Steam Ship Line, I welcome you aboard the Queen of Bermuda. If you have no immediate needs, would you please accompany me to my cabin? I must assume that, after your ordeal at sea, you might have , excuse me, some toileting needs that you can take care of in my cabin if you wish."

The group followed the Captain to a large suite near the Bridge (ship's control center). It was comfortably furnished and the Captain pointed out the bath facilities and asked that everyone be seated as soon as possible.

"As I said earlier, I am Captain Cornelius Ferrel and we are so happy to have been the ones to find you. Our late meal seating will take place in about an hour and we want you to be our guests. I have four cabins reserved for you and they are together on 'B' deck. Here are the keys. I have arranged for you to go by our gift shop immediately and pick out some light clothing there. We do not really have a clothes shop as such, but I think you can find something to

your liking there. There are dresses , slacks, and tops for
Ladies and shirts and pants for men. Most of them, I am
afraid, are emblazoned with our ship's logo but I hope you
want mind that too much. Then, if you will, freshen up –
you should have time for a quick shower – and meet me
back at this cabin when you hear the dinner bells chime
and we will order from the menu at my table. Does that
suit everyone?"

 Everyone nodded their enthusiastic approval. We have
sent messages to the Royal Navy in London indicating
your safe arrival on our ship. Am I assuming correctly that
you were enroute to the airport at Ponta Delgada?"

"That is correct, Sir", answered Henry.

"Then we will inform the chaps there of your rescue also.
We should be in Ponta Delgada at ET 6:00 A.M. That is a
regular port of call for this cruise. We will arrange
transportation to the airport and let the Royal Navy and
Ponta Delgada know of our time of arrival. I am sure that
the Royal Navy will arrange for your immediate flight to
London, either by another Navy plane or by commercial
flight. So, I will see you at dinner. A Steward will take you
to the gift shop and show you to your rooms."

They were taken to a very nice gift shop, where they were
greeted warmly by an attendant. She said, "The ladies'
wear is in this section and the men's wear is over here. Just
pick out anything you want and will feel comfortable in

while on the ship. It will be yours, of course. Also, we have some light sweaters with the ship's logo. It does get chilly at night. Please take one of them also. When you have chosen your clothing then we would like for each of you to choose two or three souvenirs to take home with you. We also have a little bag of toiletries to replace what was lost on the plane As you finish, if you will please come by my register. There is no charge but I just need to account for the merchandise in my books. And, last but not least, everyone gets one of these little canvas bags to take your things in. Of course, with our logo on the side!"

Everyone was very grateful for this thoughtful gesture. They quickly made their choices and went to the cabins for a quick shower and then, when they heard the dinner chimes, they hurried on to the Captain's table.

They had a wonderful meal with Captain Ferrel and he listened to their story of the ditching. He also raised some question that brought up how Gloria and Richard happened to be in Jamaica in the first place. Their story was so fascinating that he said, "Even though it is late and I am sure you are tired, we have a Captain's Farewell Ball at 11:00. It doesn't last very long. Would you and Richard be so kind as to give a brief presentation, perhaps twenty minutes, and include the original message and the subsequent 'speech' message. Is that asking too much, Mrs. Parsons?"

"Oh, No. We would consider it a privilege, Captain Ferrel."

Again, the presentation was received with heartfelt applause. This time, the experience that they had had in the three life rafts was added to the original story. At one point in his presentation, Richard said, "I sat in a small rubber raft, not unlike that of Jim and Melvin and Bob. I also held a glass bottle not unlike the one that Jim Stark used for his message. To make the similarity even more amazing, I was asked to take a piece of paper and write a message. But this time it was a message that led to our rescue. Yet, who is to say that Jim's message was any less liberating than mine. For his message has already lead to many changed lives, including my mother's and my own – and I hope to yours also"

Many people came up to congratulate Richard and Gloria on what they were trying to accomplish with the message in the bottle. It was a wonderful evening, in spite of all that they had gone through earlier. Gloria just wished that Leit could have been with her. Richard felt the same way.

Meanwhile, The Navy had received word of the estimated time of arrival of the survivors, and, knowing that there were also four other airmen that joined them in Bermuda, besides the ones who had flown Gloria and Richard, they decided to dispatch the newly overhauled DC4 with a fresh crew and allow the crew that were fresh from Bermuda to fly the return trip to London. The DC4 left London at

10:30 P.M, and would arrive in Ponta Delgada at 6:00 A.M.on Saturday. A shuttle would take the ten who were rescued from the steam ship docking to the airport and the DC 4 would fly back to London immediately after refueling. They should arrive in London by 3:00 in the afternoon.

Sir Thomas was apprised of all of this through his contact with the Navy. He was prepared to pick up Leit and Cassia at 6:30 on Saturday. They would eat breakfast and freshen up. Then they would have time to rest a bit before meeting the DC4 at 3:00 – If all went as planned.

.

Chapter 26. "Bless You".

There was not a lot of communication possible at this point. Leit and Cassia were in the air. Gloria and Richard had been on a raft and now were on a ship. Sir Thomas was the only one in a position to communicate. Let us look for a moment at who knew what.

As I said, Sir Thomas had the broadest view. He knew that Leit and Cassia were on the way to London and when they were expected to arrive there. He knew that Richard, Gloria, and the crew were all safe aboard a cruise ship. He knew when the ship would arrive at Ponta Delgada and that a Navy DC4 had already left to pick up the survivors and bring them back to London. He even knew that the DC4 would arrive back in London at 3:00 P.M that afternoon.

Richard and Gloria knew that they were safe. They knew that Ponta Delgada and the Royal Navy in London (and presumably Sir Thomas) had been notified of their safety. But, beyond that, they had no idea how or when they would get back to London. They did not know if Leit and Cassia even knew about the crash, much less knew that they were safe.

Leit and Cassia only knew, from the radio and T.V. News, that the plane that Richard and Gloria were on had been ditched in the ocean somewhere near the Azores. They also knew that they were in a jet plane somewhere in the dark sky and that Sir Thomas was going to meet them in London at 6:30 in the morning.

So, if knowledge equals confidence and lack of knowledge equals anxiety, then Leit and Cassia had more reason to be anxious, at least until they got to London and found out that Gloria and Richard had been rescued. Gloria and Richard had a little more knowledge but still had some reasons to be anxious. Sir Thomas, on the other hand, had a knowledge of almost all of the details, and so had very little reason to be anxious, as long as a cruise ship and two airplanes could avoid any mishaps during the next 15 or 16 hours.

In the mean time, Leit and Cassia had dinner on the plane and tried to rest or even sleep as they flew through a dark sky toward an uncertain future. They had no idea what they would learn, if anything, about the status of Gloria and Richard, when they got to London. They prayed that God would protect their loved ones on the sea.

Richard and Gloria had enjoyed a very satisfying evening, but were missing Leit and Cassia very deeply and were praying and worrying about what they were going through if they did, indeed, know about the crash. They were also trying to get some sleep, but in their waking moments they wondered how they were going to get back to London.

Sir Thomas was only wondering what all would take place between the 6:30 arrival of Leit and Cassia and the 3:00

arrival of Gloria and Richard.

At 6:30 he was standing at the proper gate at the Croydon Airport where the flight from Kingston was pulling into place. The flight was on time and he had remembered to letter a small sign, which read, LEIT AND CASSIA. The plane was very full, making him more confident that he had done the right thing in having the sign. He had always felt that such signs were somehow, well, undignified. As the crowd poured through the gate he did see an attractive woman with a 30 something male and, in his mind, elected them. He was correct. They began to smile as they approached him. Leit said, "Sir Thomas?" Sir Thomas held out his hand to Leit and shook hands but Cassia extended her hand at first and then decided to hug this man who had already meant so much to all of them.

"Oh, I must hug you, you good man! Thank you for being so kind! We would be standing here bewildered and alone, if at all, if it were not for you!"

"Come over to this bench for a moment for I have very good news," said Sir Thomas. I am sure that you have had a miserable night but that will end now." Then he filled them in on all that he knew and their smiles broadened greater and greater as he spoke. "And now," ended Sir Thomas, "The order of business is for us to get a splendid breakfast, then go to my home for you to have a nice, leisurely bath, and then we can get acquainted and you can have some much needed rest, in whatever order seems most needed at the time. How does that sound?"

"Marvelous, Sir Thomas. Thank you!" answered Cassia.

"That sounds perfect," said Leit.

"Now I will show you to the baggage area."

"Oh," said Cassia, "all we have are these two satchels, Sir Thomas. One change of clothes. You see, we had only thirty minutes to leave the house in order to connect with the flight to London."

"Of course! That is right! So we can go right on", answered Sir Thomas. "My car is just outside."

Sir Thomas went around and opened the front passenger door for Cassia and the rear door for Leit. As they drove away, Sir Thomas said, "My friends call me Thom and I would really like for you to call me that, if you will."

Leit and Cassia agreed, "Thank you!"

"Now, later on, after the stores open, if there is anything that you need – additional clothes or toiletries or anything else, just let me know and I will be glad to take you to wherever you need to go."

"Thank you for your thoughtfulness, Thom,"chimed Cassia.

They soon pulled in at "Wilmot's"

"Folks," said Thom, "You are going to have to defend yourselves. Wilmot's is known for one thing. They are dedicated to good food, but also to trying to give you more of it than you can possibly eat. They serve 'family style' so at some point you will have to choose to say, 'that's it! I can't possibly eat another bite!' Only then will they leave you alone."

"At this point," said Leit, "That sounds extremely inviting."
"To me, also," added Cassia.

They enjoyed a wonderful breakfast of big bowls of scrambled eggs, fried eggs cooked to order, bacon, ham, sausage, liver, baked beans, and waffles. They had pitchers of orange juice, milk, coffee, tea, and water on the table.

Thom, Leit, and Cassia talked about Leit and Cassia's work, education, and early days growing up. Then Thom talked about his early days in the military and his work in the government. It did unfold that both men had lost their wives at an early age.

When the meal was over, Leit excused himself and unobtrusively asked the waitress to bring the check to him. When he came back they talked further and when the check was presented to Leit , there was the inevitable battle of words and then Leit said, "Thom, you have generously given of your time, your car, and your home. You have also availed your helpful connections with the Navy. Please allow us to give you something back for the sake of our own need to do our part?"

"I see your point, very reluctantly. But I did not intend to take you out and let you pay. And this is the only time – agreed?"
"Agreed," said Leit.

They went to the English Ford and Leit and Cassia both commented about the comfort and attractiveness of the car. Thom commented on buildings and countryside as they went to his home.

After Leit and Cassia had their baths and put on their one change of clothing, Thom said, "I realize that your choice to leave last night meant that you had only minutes to pack your bags, so my offer still stands to take you by some shops if you wish to get another light change of clothing. There is a nice neighborhood department store very near here. In the mean time my clothes washer and dryer are at your disposal in a utility room next to the bathroom.

"Good," said Cassia. "I think I will wash what Leit and I wore last night. While Cassia prepared the washing, Thom showed Leit some paraphernalia from the war. When Cassia came back, she said, "If you men will excuse me, I didn't sleep too well last night and so I think I will rest for a while."

When the two men sat down, the subject of their common experiences of losing their wives came up. It was "in the back of Thom's mind" to express how much his brief acquaintance with Gloria and Richard had meant to him. He felt a friendship with Leit already and felt that he might even confide in him his hopes for a future with Gloria. But, before he had reached that point, he had asked Leit if he had ever thought of marrying again. Leit's answer changed his agenda completely.

"Well, Thom, it is interesting that you asked that question, because my answer to you, a new friend, happens to be the first time I have voiced this to anyone other than to Cassia and to Gloria. In all of these years since my wife's passing, not only have I never found another woman that I could be romantically interested in, but it has never even occurred to me to look for another. I have quite simply been too involved in my work at the Training School...until Gloria came into my office that morning.

"Since then, nothing has been the same. It still boggles my mind that in only one week's time I have fallen like some college freshman 'Lock, stock, and barrel' in love with Gloria. And the amazing thing about it is, she seems to have experienced the same thing with me! It really is difficult for me, a reasonably mature adult, to say what I am saying to another mature adult. It just sounds so crazy to speak of a serious relationship after a week. But, strangely enough, I am very sure of this and I even feel that, perhaps, it is sort of a gift of God that we have found each other."

"Well, Leit, for what it's worth to you, let me say this. I don't see it as crazy at all. I see in Gloria all of the wonderful characteristics that made me want to help her and Richard in this project that they have undertaken. I think that any man that Gloria chooses is fortunate beyond belief, and if both of you feel that you have finally found your life mate, then I feel inclined to agree that God had something to do with it!"

"Thank you, Thom. I respect your judgment and, while I honestly believe that no one on earth could change my love for Gloria, it is good to have a second opinion that my intentions, after such a short time, are not totally irresponsible."

"And do you have immediate plans, Leit?"

"I had planned to propose before Gloria left Mandeville. I began and she said she wanted to wait until we were with Richard and Cassia so that they could hear it too. So I had planned to do it in Kingston, but when we got there and I was ready to say my speech, in the course of about an hour, Cassia developed a urinary infection and we all spent the afternoon at the Emergency Room. So I still have not had the opportunity. I 'kicked myself' all night last night on the plane for not doing it before, thinking that I might never have another chance."

Meanwhile, with Gloria and Richard on the cruise ship, the ten survivors had enjoyed a light breakfast before leaving the ship. They had given their heartfelt thanks to the Captain and crew for their timely rescue and for the royal welcome that they had received. The shuttle transfer to the airport was made quickly and without incident.

They reached the DC4, which was already warming up for the flight. They went on board and renewed friendship with their original crew – Harold, Joel, Chuck, and Dennis. Then Harold introduced them to the new crew that had just flown the plane to Ponta Delgada. The Pilot was David Young, CoPilot, Andre Gopaiy, Navigator, George Gordon, and Navigator in training, Elliott Swithers, who was new on the flight team that week.

Richard and Gloria did a "double take" when they heard the name, "Swithers."

When everyone was taking their seats, Gloria and Richard sat down directly behind Elliott. After a successful take off, Gloria unfastened her seat belt and, leaning forward, tapped Elliott on his shoulder and asked, "Do you happen to have any relatives in Leeds, Elliott?"

"As a matter of fact, I do. I have a bunch of first cousins there, my mother, two uncles, and my grandfather. My father was there but he died when I was just a kid."

"Do you remember what year your father died, Elliott?"

asked Gloria.

"Well, actually, Mrs. Parsons, I don't really know if he is dead or not. You see, he was in the Navy and he disappeared in 1942."

"Oh." There was a long pause. "How should I start?" Gloria said to herself. "Please help me God, to do this right," she said, as a very sincere prayer.

"Elliott, was your father's name, Bob?"

"Yes Ma'am. He was Robert Jr., but since my grandfather was always called Robert, everyone called my father, Bob."

"It is sort of a long story, Elliott. We have planned to go to Leeds either tomorrow or Monday, to share that story with your family. It looks like you are going to be the first one in your family to hear it, and that is very appropriate, since you are Bob's son. The story that my son is going to share with you and your family is sad. But I hope that it will also give you relief" Gloria could tell that Elliott's face showed a mixture of fear and anticipation. He was probably bracing himself for "the worst".

"Elliott, your Dad did die in 1942 and our story will explain how we know that he died.."

Tears filled the young man's eyes, but he also smiled. "Oh,

God. You don't know how much relief it would bring to my family, especially to my mother and Grandpa, to know what really happened to my father. The whole family has had this whole big area of our lives that has always been temporary and tentative with no finality. Any time my father's name is mentioned, it is followed by, 'wherever he is' or 'if he is still living', or we will do this or that 'some day if your father comes back'. If you can tell us what happened to my father it will be the most wonderful gift you could ever give anybody!"

"Elliott. We have been in Jamaica, telling this story to another family that was involved. We will tell it to you just as we told it to them. With your permission I will invite these other gentlemen to sit where they can hear this story. Is that OK with you?"

"Yes Ma'am, I want them to hear it."

Gloria raised her voice - "Gentlemen, if you wish to hear this true story. It concerns Elliott's Dad, who served in the Royal Navy and gave his life for his country in 1942. He was reported missing in action and his family has not heard anything about him during these years, because no one knew what happened to him until now. My son has some information that he wants to share with Elliott and with you this morning. I know that you will respect the importance of this experience for him."

Richard told the story just as he had done before. He then related the experience that he had had in his own life raft, feeling some of the same feelings that those three men must have felt during those twenty days in 1942.

Gloria decided not to go into the part about Dr. Dorster's speech, thinking that it might detract from the central purpose of the moment. She simply said that they had already shared the message with the loved ones of Jim Stark and Melvin Dorster. Now they planned to go to Leeds and speak with Elliott's family. Gloria said that they would be going to Leeds either on Sunday or Monday.

Elliott said, "I would certainly like to be there when you go, if I can get off. My instructor is a good guy and I think he will give me a couple of days off when I tell him why."

"I will give you two phone numbers," said Gloria. "One is my home phone and the other is Commander Lawn. If you keep trying at these numbers you should be able to reach me sooner or later. Then I can tell you when we will be going. Do you have a car?"

"Yes Ma'am."

"I do have one question, Elliott," said Gloria. "Commander Lawn has tried for a week to find your father's name in the Navy records and could not. He thinks that, perhaps, his records were on the ship that went down. But I wonder why your name would not have appeared?"

"Well, Ma'am, I have had a 'mix up' with my name ever since I joined the Navy, and that is just a few weeks. They somehow typed it up as 'Smithers', and that is the way it went into the Navy's records. They just got it straight a few days ago."

One of the crewmen had glanced out the window and noticed an unusual amount of black smoke coming out of one of the engines. "Hey, guys, number 3 engine looks strange, look at that smoke! You guys that flew it down, did it look like that then?"

David, the pilot who brought it down, said, "It's OK. The mechanics told me that they replaced some parts in number 3 and that it would smoke more than usual for a few days and then it would smooth out. I'll go tell Henry so they won't worry."

Gloria looked at Richard and they both said, "Whew!"

During the next several hours, Gloria talked some more to Elliott. Elliott also talked with Richard about the details of his finding the bottle and his subsequent feelings when he was in his own little rubber raft in the middle of the ocean. At noon time, someone passed out some cookies and other goodies that Captain Ferrel had thoughtfully sent along.

Finally, at 2:45, Harold said, "fifteen minutes until touch down. Be thinking about getting your seat belts on and fastened!"

At 3:00, the DC4 was rolling to a stop at its proper gate. Richard and Gloria were hoping that Thom would know to be there and that he would have had some sort of contact with Leit and Cassia so they would not be worried – if they even knew about the crash at all.

When Richard and Gloria came down the ramp and saw Leit and Cassia, they took off in a full run. They could not get there fast enough. There was a spontaneous four way hug. Thom was amazed as he looked on.

Leit suddenly got down on one knee and said, "Gloria Parsons, I had a wonderful speech that I was going to say, but I have forgotten the whole thing except that I love you very much and I don't want to live another day without you. Will you marry me and be my wife forever and ever? Please? That's not very pretty, but it sure is from my heart!"

Thom said, "By all means say 'yes', Gloria! This man loves you! He really does!"

Gloria looked at Thom in complete surprise and then looked into Leit's eyes and placed her hands on his shoulders. With a smile on her face and a heart full of joy, she said, "Oh, Yes, Leit! Yes! Yes! Yes! I love you and I don't want to live another day without you either!"

With that, Thom lifted his right hand in a pontifical gesture and said, "Bless You! Bless You! Bless You!". He then entered into a five way hug that lasted for a very long time. A hundred bystanders, who had witnessed the whole scene, gave a "standing ovation"!

Chapter 27. "Unfinished Business".

Several of the bystanders came by to congratulate Gloria and Leit. When all of the excitement died down, Thom suggested they go out to the car and decide what their schedule needed to be. They walked out to the English Ford and Thom apologized that it was not large enough to hold all of them comfortably. "I am afraid that someone will have to sit on someone's lap. "I think we can handle that," laughed Leit. So, Richard got in the front with Thom, Cassia got in the back, and Leit sat in the back on the other side. Gloria snuggled into Leit's lap.

"Is everyone comfortable?" asked Thom

"Very!" laughed Gloria.

"Absolutely!" agreed Leit.

"Now, I need to ask a question about priorities, Gloria, and I have no preference. First, do you have anything that needs immediate consideration - do you need to check where you work, for instance? Do you need to check by your house? Or, is there anything else?"

Gloria responded, "Sooner or later we will need to stop by a restroom, but it isn't an emergency. We need to talk a bit about all that has happened, so why don't we go by my house. I can check the house and the car. We can have some refreshments and talk around our trusty kitchen table.

I can call my Broker and just let him know that I am back and see how soon I can talk with him about my plans, which you may or may not know about, Thom"

"Dear, Cassia and I felt that you should be the one to fill Thom in on that! I did give him a preview of my plans to propose to you when you arrived, so he might have assumed that you would be going to Jamaica."

"OK," said Thom. "Now I do not know how big your house is, Gloria, but I have four bedrooms that you are certainly welcome to use."

"That is very kind of you, Thom," said Gloria, but we do have three bedrooms and a 'sleep away sofa' and that should take care of everyone. But let's do go over there now and get our story all 'out on the table'. I have coffee, tea, and fizz pop in the house."

So they went across to Gloria's house, just a few miles from the airport. When they got there, Richard checked the car, a 1951 Vauxhall Velox. It was secure and started immediately. That was a relief. Gloria invited everyone in and said, "If anyone needs to use the bathroom, it is down the hall to the left. Then come out and we'll sit at the kitchen table. Who wants what to drink?" Everyone wanted tea, so she put on some water to boil. "Everyone, please be comfortable. Let me call my Broker. It shouldn't take but a few minutes. She was back in less than five minutes. "My Broker is going to make it easy for me. He is coming by here tonight at 9:00. He knows that I am moving so he will bring the contract for me to sign as an absentee seller. That will definitely free up tomorrow!"

Richard said, "Mom, I think it would be an interesting thing if we just quickly went through all of the happenings from the finding of the message in the bottle until this very moment. We could just sort of 'brain storm' it and everybody could just add to or ask questions. How about that?"

"That is a terrific idea, Richard. Just everyone jump in with what you know and ask questions if you wish. OK, I guess Richard and I will lead off."

"Richard found the bottle while he was fishing, brought it home, He read it to Gloria. They decided to search for survivors of the three men. They found a former address of Jim Stark, through Thom. Met Betsey, at that address. She told them how to get in touch with Clara Woolsey, who was planning to marry Jim. They read the message to Clara and Betsey."

"They found, through a letter from Jim to Clara, that Melvin Dorster was not only a sailor but a former professor at a school of higher education in Jamaica. They called The West Indian Training School, as one of the possibilities, and found that, not only was Dr. Dorster formerly a professor there but his brother is currently a professor there. Thom arranged for them to fly to Jamaica and Gloria made an appointment with Dr. Leitman Dorster for two days hence. Not only did they have an appointment with him, but that afternoon they went on his schooner and told their story to students and faculty on the ship. During the next week, Richard and Gloria told their story, with Leit's help, at least 9 different times - on a sailboat, schools, a church, a legislature house, a cruise ship, an airplane, and you might even count a life raft."

"On the way back to London, they crashed in the ocean. Thom was notified and Leit and Cassia heard about it over the radio. They called Thom and he said he would meet their plane in London. They got on a Jet, not knowing whether Gloria and Richard had perished or been rescued. A cruise ship rescued Richard and Gloria. They told their story to the Captain and he asked them to repeat the story at the Captain's Farewell Ball later in the evening. The Navy flew a plane to get the survivors in Ponta Delgada."

"On the way back, Gloria found out that one of the crewmen that brought the DC4 to Ponta Delgada, was a new navigator student, Elliott Swithers, the son of Bob Swithers. Thom met Leit and Cassia at the airport and all three later met Gloria and Richard at the Navy Airport. Leit proposed in a spectaculor way in front of hundreds of bystanders. Gloria said, 'Yes' after Thom said, 'You'd better!' Then Thom blessed them and here we all are! Whew!"

"Somebody should write that up!" joked Gloria.

"Somebody probably will," said Thom. "I have made a proposal to the Navy and have received a tentative approval for this: If Gloria and Richard will write up something similar to what we have just heard, with a few more details, of course, the Navy will fly Gloria and Richard - and now Cassia and Leit I am sure - back to Kingston. They will also take up to two trunks and two suitcases. How about that?"

"Oh, that would be great fun, Thom. You are such a great man, Thom. We can't thank you enough!" This was Gloria's response but the others were all agreeing with words and nodding heads.

"Well, just consider that a wedding present! Now I propose that we all go out to eat. Do you have a favorite place, Gloria and Richard?'

"Well, Leit and Cassia are used to the great seafood of Jamaica. I think we should show them that London also has some pretty good seafood too. How about Hobson's?"

"Great choice. Does seafood meet everyone's approval?' Everyone shook their heads in the affirmative. "Hobson's it is, then! If we leave here in about 30 minutes, that will be 6:00. That would allow a leisurely dinner and time to go by the grocer before your appointment with your Broker at 9:00."

"OK, now one other thing," said Gloria. "Are we talking

about a Wednesday morning flight like it was before, and, if so, would it be this Wednesday?"

"It can be this Wednesday or any Wednesday that you wish, Gloria."

"So, let me try to call Mr. Swithers in Leeds and see what we can arrange so that we will know something when Elliott calls. Everyone just be comfortable for a few minutes"

As Gloria was walking toward the telephone, it rang. It was Elliott. He had already talked with his grandfather. The grandfather wanted to know if they could come down tomorrow. If they could, it would be a lot easier to get everyone together on Sunday. He would like to have everyone down there for a dinner in the park.

"Would it be OK if we brought three other people who were involved in the story?" Gloria asked.

"Oh, Yes Ma'am, by all means!"

"Then, let me check." Gloria asked everyone and they said,"Yes."
"Now, it takes three hours, right," asked Gloria.

Yes, Ma'am, and, if you need to spend the night, they have plenty of room."

"Where should we meet you?" asked Gloria.

"There is a big restaurant, McKinley's, just before you go onto Highway M1 going North. If we meet there at 8:30 tomorrow morning, that would put us at the the picnic before 12:00, and don't bring a thing but your appetite!"

"We know where McKinley's is located. Will you be by yourself?"

"Yes Ma'am."

"We have a problem with space. Both of our cars are four passenger but there are five of us. Could one of us get in with you?"

"How about if Richard rides with me?"

"That would be perfect, Elliott. When do you need to be back to your quarters?"

"Well, I will need to be back tomorrow night at 9:00 P.M."

"That's good, if we all left at about 4:00, would that be too early?"

"No, that sounds just right to me!"

"OK," said Gloria. "So we will see you tomorrow morning at 8:30 at McKinley's. What color is your car?"

"It is a cherry red 1951 MGTD."

"You will go with the speed limit, won't you Elliott?"
"That depends on you, Mrs. Parsons. I am going to drive in
back of your car and if you race I guess I will have to race
to keep up!" They both had a laugh with that one.

"Give us a number where we can reach you if I need to,
Elliott.l"

"It's 625-3528, Ma'am."

Before Thom left Gloria's, they decided to meet at
McKinley's for breakfast at 7:00. Gloria called Elliott back
and he said he would be there at 7:00 too. Thom would
meet them there and they would go in the English Ford,
since it was a little newer than Gloria's car. They would
leave the Vauxhall at McKinley's.

Gloria's Broker was right on time and stayed about 45
minutes. Before that Gloria had asked Cassia to take one of
the extra bedrooms and Leit, the other one. Richard was
glad to sleep on the "make - a - bed sofa". Everyone was
worn out so they went to bed shortly after the Broker left.

The next morning, when Gloria pulled up to the restaurant
and saw the red car she said, "Richard, he's driving a sports
car!"

"Sure, Mom. Didn't you know that an MGTD is a sports

car?"

"No! Well, I guess it will be OK. Don't let him drive too fast!"

"I won't Mom.'

Everyone had a moderate breakfast because they had been warned by Elliott that his folks didn't know when to stop when it came to picnics."

During the trip there was wonderful conversation. They asked questions about the experience in the life boats and their time on the cruise ship. Gloria told them about her discovering that Elliott was Bob Swithers' son. They even questioned Gloria and Leit about any plans for the wedding. Leit said, "We haven't had time to discuss the wedding, but I hope that it will be as soon as possible. I know that I am being selfish at that point. You will certainly be invited, Thom."

"Well, who knows. I might be able to hitch a ride on a Navy plane if you plan it on a Thursday!"

"We will certainly keep that in mind, Thom," said Gloria.

They all arrived safely at the picnic at exactly 12:00 noon. Elliott drove behind Thom and let him set the pace, to Gloria's relief. Elliott got out first and the whole clan came over at once. They lined up respectfully - grandfather, mother, the two sons and their wives, followed by all of the cousins and their wives and families. All in all there were at least 20 of the Swithers family there.

They, of course, had a buffet. They placed the guests in the honored chairs in the middle of the table. Gloria had told Thom that they planned to do the presentation pretty much as they had been doing it during the last week. They did honor Thom in a special way. Gloria thanked him because the success of the whole effort was largely because of Thom's help. Leit said that he owed Thom a special debt of gratitude because if it had not been for Thom's help, he would never have even met his bride to be. After telling the story as they had been doing, Gloria used the notes that she had made at the table on Saturday night to give a very quick review of all that had happened from the very beginning until that very minute.

After the presentation, Mr. Robert Swithers, the grandfather, stood and told in very tearful but happy words, how much this new knowledge about his son had helped him. Then the mother gave a similar personal testimony. Each of the brothers had a word. Some of the cousins added their feelings also. Elliott repeated pretty much what he had said on the plane to Gloria. The tone of the whole family was that this would give them a new lease on life and free them from a sort of ghost like uncertainty that had haunted their lives for all of these twelve years.

Everything about the experience was satisfying and Richard and Gloria both felt that they had carried out their unspoken promise to the three men in that little life raft. Of course the whole family would now extend the thrust of Dr. Melvin Dorster's speech, as they go back to Mandeville and work toward the establishment of the university. The message in the bottle had now worked its wonderful magic completely and now it could be retired. Gloria would have a facsimile prepared and one sent to everyone involved.

By the way, when she met with her Broker at 9:00 the previous night, he told her that, as a wedding present to Gloria and Leit, he would personally see that their house was cleaned and that any little thing that needed painting or repair would be put in first class order. He would also encourage the showing and sale of the house just as if it were his own personal home. In addition, he would keep the car at the office, advertise it regularly until it sold, and get the very best price he could possible get for it.

It appears that Gloria, Leit, Richard, and Aunt Cassia could easily be ready to leave on the DC4 - with 4 engines - on Wednesday morning at 6:00 A.M.

Chapter 28. "Going Home".

Richard rode back with Elliott and everyone met at the same restaurant. Elliott had let Richard drive the MG part of the way back and Richard was "ruined for life". "Some day," he said, "I will have an MGTD. It might take twenty years, but I will have one!" They got back home at about 7:30 and Gloria fixed a light, very light, supper.

There were two things that Gloria wanted to do before leaving London. She would like for Cassia and Leit to meet Clara and Betsey. She also wanted them to see their own beach at Brighton Beach, and go out in the boat to where Richard found the bottle. She would call Clara and see which day would be best for her and then go to Brighton Beach on the other day.

 She called Betsey and she was delighted to hear from Gloria again. She said she would love to see Clara and either day would be fine. She called Clara and Clara said, "Either day would be fine, but the sooner the better! Please plan to get here about 12:00 and we will take a long lunch break. We'll have lunch for you in my apartment upstairs."

"So let's make it tomorrow, then, O.K.?"said Gloria.

"I'll look for you then, Gloria!"

Gloria called back and made the date with Betsey. " We will pick you up at 10:45 in the morning!"

Gloria outlined her plan to Leit, Cassia, and Richard and everyone agreed. She decided to begin getting things ready for the trip back to Jamaica so she went down to the basement and found the old but sturdy trunk, that had been a storage compartment for years. She took everything out and vacuumed it clean. She called Richard downstairs and said, "Richard, we need to pack light for our move. We have this one trunk and we can get another one if we really need it. But, if possible, I'd like to stick with one trunk and two suit cases. Do you think that is doable?"

"It's worth a try, Mom!"

"So, you see the things I took out. How about looking through those and then look around the basement. Take this box and put anything you really want to take with us. We will box up the other things and take them to the Charity Bazaar Association."

"Ok, Mom."

"I will go up to my room and put all the things I can't part with and put them in this other box. We will see what we have after the process is over," added Gloria.

Gloria went all over the house, gathering pictures, books, and memories. She added a few sweaters and English wool items and took everything to the basement. When she had combined her choices with Richards, she was surprised that there would still be a little room for last minute additions. It truly appeared that one trunk would suffice. Her clothes, after carefully sorting out what she would never need in Jamaica, would fit in her one large suit case. Richard's would fit in the other. They would finish boxing up everything else for the Charity Association in their spare time Monday and Tuesday. They were very surprised at how little time it had taken to decide what was truly important in their lives.

Everyone was ready to go to bed early. It had been a very full day. Leit and Gloria decided to take a little walk because they had not had much private time together since they all got to London. "Let's think a little about our ideas for the wedding", said Gloria, "and see if our thoughts are similar or not. I do not want to rush you or anything, but if one of us is thinking a year and one of us is thinking a week, then we need to know that, OK?"

"Darling," said Leit, "my thinking is very definite and has been at least since you went down in the ocean and probably even before that. I would like for us to be married as soon as we can make arrangements that satisfy you. I know that engagement periods are the usual practice and if you would feel more comfortable setting the wedding date several months away, then I don't mind that. But I am ready to set the date as soon as possible. If you would like to have more time for any reason, then that will be OK. For me, I was thinking that there are two possibilities. You can come and live with us until you find a rental house or apartment and then stay there for the duration of our engagement and then, I am assuming, you would be willing to live in my present house. Cassia is quite willing to rent or buy a house and move at whatever time is convenient for us. The other possibility is for us to plan our wedding as soon as possible and you simply live at our house and not look for an intermediate housing. In that case, Cassia would begin to look for another house immediately."

"Dear Leit. I believe that engagement periods are primarily for young people who are lacking in experience in knowing their feelings and in what marriage is all about. Neither one of those categories fits us. I know that I love you and I am confident that you love me. I know how to have a good marriage and I believe that you do too. So I really do not see any value in arbitrarily deciding to wait. I would feel inclined to decide where we want our wedding and go see the minister as soon as we get back home. When I said, 'where' I was assuming that the Anglican Church in Mandeville would be the most likely location, but I did not want to rule out an outside location like 'our hill top' if you felt so inclined."

"Wow, I am overwhelmed with joy," said Leit. "You see it just as I do. So that's what I would like to do, go see Rev. Bernard immediately and I really do like the idea of the wedding on the hill top. The only problem I can foresee is space. I think that there could easily be 250 people attending. I can picture us standing lower than the audience, with them looking down on the ceremony. Let's look at that as soon as we get home and decide. So, are we talking about a week or so after we get back?"

"Yes. Let us say as soon as Rev. Bernard can work it into his schedule, AND, since Thom has already said that he could come if we have it on a Thursday, I think we should make every effort to have it then. I also think we should be careful not to give Cassia any pressure at all to move before she can comfortably find another home."

"I appreciate your thoughtfulness about that and I know she will too."

"I guess we had better be getting back home," said Gloria. Richard and Cassia will be wondering about us."

While Gloria and Leit were walking, Cassia and Richard were enjoying their first private time together since they had been in London. They were both sitting in the living room. "Aunt Cassia, I don't want to put you on the spot, but are you feeling OK about Mother and Dr. Dorster?"

"Ha! You are going to have to decide what you are comfortable calling my brother, aren't you? But we can come back to that. I am very happy about them being together. I would say that they are both very lucky, but I don't think luck had anything to do with it. I honestly believe that, whatever powers that be in Heaven brought these two together. I know Leit and he is a really good man. I've seen your mother enough to know that she is a wonderful woman and I believe that each is exactly what the other one has needed. So, how do you feel about it?"

"Exactly the same as you do, Aunt Cassia. Exactly the same. Besides that, I needed and Aunt like you!"
" You are perfect for me, too!" Cassia gave Richard a big hug and he adored it.

"Now," asked Richard, "What would you suggest that I call your brother?"

"My very best choice, knowing him as I do, is this. I don't know how you feel about the term 'Dad'. Maybe you feel that it is only appropriate for your biological father. Or maybe you would feel it would somehow be disloyal to your father. But, if you could be comfortable using the term, 'Dad', then I would suggest you do this: Go to him and say that you want him to be comfortable with what you call him, but, if it is OK, that you would really like to call him 'Dad'. I think he would love that and it would definitely get you both off to a good start!"

"That really is what I would like, Aunt Cassia. That is exactly how I will go about it. Thank you so much."

On Monday morning they got up and ate breakfast at 7:30. Then Richard and Gloria picked up some more things for the Charity Association. They were determined that they would have everything in the house either in the trunk and suit cases to take to Mandeville or else in the boxes labeled

"Charity Association". Gloria felt that they could take everything on Tuesday afternoon, even if it took two trips. There was a place where they could leave their trunk and suit cases at the airport on Tuesday evening and they would put them on the plane on Wednesday morning. Then, on Wednesday morning Gloria would drive her car and leave it at the real estate office and drop the key in a "drop box". Gloria had already left the necessary papers with her Broker that would allow him to sell the car for her. Then, Thom would pick them up at the real estate office at 5:15 and take them directly to the plane.

But on Monday morning, at 10:45, they picked up Betsey. They decided to let Leit drive and Gloria sit in the front to direct. Richard, Cassia, and Betsey would try to squeeze in the back seat. If that were too tight, they would try putting the three women in the back seat. That is the way they finally had to work it out. They got to Guildford at exactly 12:00 noon. When they went into the shop, Charley greeted them with a big smile on his face. "Hey, Mrs. Parsons! Hi – you are Richard, right? And....? "Charley, I want you to meet my 'husband to be' Leit Dorster, and his sister, Cassia. And you know Betsey, I believe."

"Yes Ma'am, I know that nice lady! And I'm glad to know you, Cassia and Leit. I want to thank you, Mrs. Parsons, because you and Richard made it possible that I hope to be what Leit is – that 'husband to be'."

"Are they here?" yelled Clara from upstairs.

"Yes, they are!" Charley yelled back.

"Well, lock the door and bring them upstairs!"

They all clomped up the stairs and Clara hugged Gloria, Richard, and Betsey and said, "this must be your 'husband to be'!"

"Yes, Clara, this is Leit and his sister, Cassia."

"Well, everybody just sit down at the table and I've got something I hope you will like."

Clara brought out: Roast lamb, carrots, peas, Bubble and squeak (a traditional English recipe with potatoes, cabbage fried with onions), broccoli - cheese bake, Yorkshire pudding, and an assortment of Clara's and Charley's favorite cookies from the shop.

After the meal, everyone went into the living room and, after everyone had settled in their chairs, Clara said, "OK. I know that you went to Jamaica, so tell me all about it!"

"Well, there isn't much to tell except that I went down there, fell in love, and now I am about to get a new husband, a new sister, and a new home – all at the same time!"

"Well, I've always heard that the Jamaica sand has some

sort of magical property that does strange things to visitors."

"Seriously, though, Clara, the information you gave us, from Jim's letter, about Dr. Melvin Dorster's speech, worked wonders. There is a strong campaign, already mounting, to build the school that we visited into a four year university. Then Gloria and Richard told the whole story about the flight and about their week in Jamaica. When they finished, they said, "Now, Clara, tell us what is new with you."

"Well, surprisingly enough, I have had my own adventure right here in my little Cookie Shop. If you noticed the new smile on my face, it is because I have discovered a diamond right here in my own back yard. Thanks to your message from Jim, I felt free to actually look at Charley, here, in a whole new light. I liked him before, but I never allowed myself to see him in a romantic way before now. I suppose the same thing happened to Charley and me that happened to you and Leit, Gloria. It just goes to show you that sometimes it doesn't take a lot of time. Of course, Betsey kind of egged me on too!"
"That I did!" confessed Betsey.

"So, Charley has made a double proposal. First we will get married and move into his house. Then he will pool his savings with mine and we will remodel the Cookie Shop and add a tea room up here. He will manage the tea room until it is going good and then we will train another

manager up here and he will come back down with me
again."

Everyone enjoyed the afternoon and then at about 3:00,
Gloria told Clara and Charley that she had some things to
finish up for them to be ready to leave early Wednesday
morning, so they would need to be going. She said that
they would keep in touch and they exchanged addresses
and telephone numbers before they left.

As they traveled back to London, Leit commented that it
had been a wonderful experience for he and Cassia to have
touched on the results of all of the contacts that the
message in the bottle had made. Also, he had been able to
sense the tremendous difference that the message had
made in the lives of so many people.

The rest of the evening was spent finishing up the final
touches to the house and its contents. Gloria called her
friend that had the cottage in Brighton Beach and gave her
a report of all that had happened and asked for permission
to use the cottage, briefly, just one more time. She donated
the boat for the use of the cottage and thanked her for
sharing the cottage all of these years.

The next morning, they had a leisurely breakfast and drove
down to Brighton Beach. Since the cottage was only a five
minute bike ride from the dock where the boat was tied,
Gloria and Leit used the two bicycles and rode to the
beach, while Cassia and Richard drove. Since the boat

would only hold two people safely, Richard took Cassia first to show her exactly where he found the bottle. Gloria and Leit rode the bikes up the road that followed the beach. She showed him the unusual houses on the beach. Then they came back and Gloria showed Leit the boat route while Richard and Cassia rode the bikes. It was a really nice afternoon and the smell of the ocean was very refreshing to everyone. Gloria said, "very soon we will be able to smell these breezes every day!"

Seeing the actual spot where the bottle was found and realizing the distance that the bottle had been carefully guided and protected in its travels, convinced both Leit and Cassia that there was a Divine hand involved. This seemed especially true when they were reminded that Richard was quite ready to go home when he felt the sudden, overwhelming urge to go to the marker where the bottle was floating.

After going back to London, they put the boxes in the car and took them to the Charity Association. It took them two trips for that. Then they came back and took the trunk and the two suit cases to the airport. The trunk fit into the back of the Vauxhall only by leaving the boot (trunk) open and temporarily removing the back seat.

They all went to bed early and had a good breakfast the next morning. They were not taking a lunch this time because they learned on the last trip that if they waited a little past lunch time they could get a wonderful meal at their first refueling stop in the Azores.

They met Thom at the real estate office and dropped off the car and the keys. Thom took them to the airport, where they were reunited with their crew: David, the pilot; Andre, the co-pilot; George, the Navigator; and Elliott, the Student Navigator. They said a final 'thank you' to Thom and everyone gave him a warm hug. It was not the kind of hug he had originally hoped for from Gloria, but he would settle for seeing her happy.

Gloria, Richard, Leit, and Cassia filled out their mandatory forms, took their seats in the plane, and relaxed. Gloria thought of their baggage and asked David if he was sure the trunk was on board. He said, "Yes Ma'am, I checked the trunk and the two suit cases personally. They are definitely going to Jamaica!"
Gloria looked at Leit and smiled. "WE are going to Jamaica! WE are GOING HOME."

As the airplane gained speed down the runway, Gloria reached over and gripped Leit's hand. "I love the feel of your hand, Leit – and will love it for the rest of my life!"

Chapter 29. "Follow Your Dream"

The trip back to Jamaica was uneventful. Leit enjoyed the interaction with the crew. He was especially glad to see Elliott again.

Gloria began to think about details. "Leit, how can we possibly get that trunk into the Nash to go to Mandeville?"

"That is no problem, Dear," said Leit. "We will treat it as furniture. We will go by a furniture hauling company. We give them our name and address and tell them exactly where to pick up the trunk. We give them a deposit and they go by and pick it up at the airport and store it temporarily until the next full load goes to Mandeville, which should be within a few days. Then they will bring the trunk to our house and we pay the balance. That is all there is to it."

"I would not have known how to do that, Leit. You are so smart!"

"You are just prejudiced," laughed Leit.

They went to the same restaurant in the Azores and the food was wonderful. Since they would not be near a refueling stop at supper time, and Gloria had not brought a lunch as before, Leit ordered sandwiches for everyone for later in the evening.

The passengers all slept well on the plane, after eating the sandwiches – much better than Leit and Cassia had slept on their flight to London. When they got to Kingston, the second crew took them to where their trunk would be taken and they found out the exact location to give to the furniture movers. Then one of the crew members took them to their car at the other airport. Gloria, again, was "forced" to sit on Leit's lap. When they were in Leit's Nash, they found a restaurant and got a really big breakfast. They were quite hungry after having the sandwiches for supper. They took their time eating because it was still early and the furniture movers would not open until 8:00. At 8:00 they were sitting in front of the movers that had been recommended at the airport. They made the necessary arrangements and were on the road by 8:30. It really felt good to be on the way to Mandeville again At 9:00, Leit said, "It was just about this time two weeks ago when Rachel brought you two into my office and introduced you to Cassia and me. It is like another world has come into my life since then!"

"Me too," said Gloria.

"Yep," agreed Richard.

"Absolutely," said Cassia.

They arrived in Mandeville about 11:30. "What would you like to do about lunch?" asked Leit.

"This might sound rather bold," said Gloria, "but I would like to have Cassia show me around the kitchen and then let me help her get some lunch on the table at our new home. It is so good to be here! I can not tell you how really good this feels!"

"I will be happy to do that, Gloria. Will sandwiches be OK just for today? If so, we will need to go by the grocer and get some milk, bread, cheese, and sandwich meat."

"Yes. That is another area that Cassia can orient me to - if it is any different from those in London."

"Then let's get started. Drop us off at Manworth's, Leit.

"I'll walk over and get a newspaper while you two go in. Want to come with me, Richard?"

"Yes, Sir." Richard was quiet as they walked to the news stand and back. When they got back to the car, Richard said, "Sir, I feel a bit awkward calling you Dr. Dorster. It isn't so bad now, but after you and Mom are married I don't think Dr. Dorster will work very well. I was wondering what you would feel most comfortable with, Sir?"

"Richard, I appreciate your asking, but I will only feel comfortable if I know that you are using the term that satisfies your needs the best. What would you really like to call me?"

"I've been without a father for a long time and I have missed having a Dad. I would really like to think of you as my father in every way possible. I can not change the fact that you are not my biological father but in every other way I would like to think of you as my father. I would like to call you 'Dad', if you don't mind."

Tears came into Leit's eyes and he hugged Richard to his chest and said, "I will be very honored to be your father in every way and for you to be my son in every way. It will make me very happy if you will call me 'Dad'."

When Cassia and Gloria came back, Richard announced, "Dad and I have decided that I can retire the term, Dr. Dorster, except for the very most formal occasions and I will just call him 'Dad'."

"Good for you both!" said Gloria. "I hope that any problem we ever have can be solved that quickly and efficiently. I think that calls for a four way hug when we get home."

They went home and went directly to the kitchen, where Cassia gave a quick walking tour of the pantry, the overhead cabinets, and an orientation of the stove and refrigerator. After a really tasty lunch, Gloria said, "Now for that four way hug, but before that I want to give a quick speech. Cassia, this has been your home with Leit for several years. It would hurt me deeply if I thought that my coming here would hurt you in any way or that you would ever see me as a competitor with you. If at some time in the future you choose to find another home, let it be of your own choosing and not because you do not feel welcome here. With that said, let's Father, Mother, Son, Sister, Aunt have a big, big, hug together!"

"Now, your father and I have some business up on the hill, but we would welcome the opinion of the whole family, so if you would all come with me. Yes, I have an idea that Richard has a telephone call that he is anxious to make, but please just give us ten minutes. I think that is all that it will take. When they got to the top of the hill, Leit said, "Now, we have two alternatives for our wedding. The Anglican Church, of course, but also this hill top has been a significant place for Gloria and me. We are trying to decide if there is a way that up to 250 people would be able to stand comfortably for 45 minutes and be able to see the ceremony. Would it be best if the ceremony were at the top and the audience lower or would it be best for the ceremony to be lower and the audience above?"

Richard said, "Personally, I think that if the ceremony were at the very top and the audience circled the ceremony like a theater in the round, with just one path through which the wedding party would enter, then I think there would be plenty of room for 250.

"I agree, said Cassia – no doubt in my mind."

"I think that will work perfectly," said Gloria. "I really

do!"

"Then that is what we will do," said Leit.

"I would be very honored if you, Cassia, will be my Maid of Honor!"
"Oh, Yes. Gloria. Thank you! Yes! That would be so wonderful!" said Cassia.
" I would not want anyone else to be my Best Man than my son, Richard!"
"I will be happy to, Dad!"

"One more thing," said Gloria, Gabi and Consuela will also be in our wedding, I hope. Either both will be flower girls or Gabi will be flower girl and Consuela will be the ring bearer – can a girl do that? We'll ask Rev. Burnett about that."

"Why don't we pay the Reverend a visit right now, Gloria? I guess we should call first to see if it is convenient for him. Then, Richard, if you want to, call Jacqueline and see if you want us to drop you off."

Leit found that the Reverend would be at home in two hours and that the housekeeper would tell him that Leit and Gloria would be coming after 4:00. Richard called and said that Jacqueline was home and anxious to see him, so Leit gave him the keys to the Nash and asked him to please have it back by 4:00 or shortly after. Richard thanked him and agreed about the time.

Leit put another Rachmaninoff on the player and Gloria recognized it as the third movement of his Second Piano Concerto."You really are good, Mrs. Dorster to be!"

"Thank you, my hubby to be! Now, I have a piece of paper. We need to make a list so we won't forget anything when we talk with the Reverend."

Items for the Reverend

Can he officiate at an outdoor wedding?

Does he think we can do it outdoors if there are 250 people there?

Go over the wedding service that he uses.

What do we need to do to be married? License, Blood test, etc.

Can a little girl be a ring bearer?

His fees.

"Can you think of anything else?"asked Gloria. "Oh. Would you want to make up any of the service ourselves?"

"Yes. I would l like that very much.."

Richard drove up just before 4:00. He was radiant with

happiness.

Leit and Gloria drove over to the Parish House and found Rev. Burnett to be home and expecting them.

After introductory remarks, Rev. Burnett ushered Leit and Gloria into his study. "I am so glad to see that you are back so soon from London, " said Rev. Burnett.

Leit and Gloria gave a brief review of all that had happened to them, and ended with a request that he perform their wedding.

Rev. Burnett said, "Leit and Gloria, I am honored that you have asked me to be a part of this happy event. If you were younger, I would usually suggest a series of sessions of marriage preparation but I think that would be like bringing coals to New Castle. I believe that both of you have been married and are both mature, experienced adults who know what is involved in a happy marriage. If I remember correctly you both have lost spouses by death.

I will give you the address where you may obtain a marriage license. You will need to take with you a notarized copy of your proof of citizenship and a copy of the death certificate of your spouse. There is no blood test required. Any questions so far?"

"We have a list, so let me go over those quickly so you will know our concerns. We are considering an outdoor wedding up on a hill that is in back of our house. The view is spectacular. Would you consider that?"

"Oh yes. I love outdoor weddings. Just be sure that you have an alternative plan in case of rain. The Church would be available for that."

"If there are 250 people there, would the outdoors work?"

"Yes. We have a portable P.A. System that projects beautifully."

"We wanted to write part of our vows to make it more personal. Would that be OK?"

"Yes. I will give you a copy of our usual Anglican Wedding Ceremony and at one point I will inject a question, such as, 'What expressions of your devotions to each other would you like to make to your friends and loved ones who are gathered here today?"
"OK," said Gloria, "There are two little girls that I would like to have a part in the ceremony. I would like for one to be a flower girl and one to be a ring bearer. Is it OK to have a girl ring bearer?"

"Sure. It is perfectly OK. Plan to have a brief rehearsal a couple of days before, so that everyone will know what to do and when."

"Now, Rev. Burnett, we really did not have any reason to

put off our wedding. We would like to have it on a Thursday so that someone special will be able to attend. When would be the first time that you would have a free Thursday within the next two or three weeks.?"

"Let me look at my calendar. Today is August 5. The 12th I am out of town. I am free on the next Thursday. That is August 19. How about that?"

"August 19. That sounds wonderful. Would 7:00 give us enough daylight? It would allow people time to get home from work. How would you suggest we invite people when there is not enough time to send out a large group of invitations?"

"I would suggest that you send out invitations to your close friends and put an invitation on the social page of the newspaper to 'All of our Friends'," suggested Rev. Burnett.

"Then could we have the rehearsal on Tuesday, the 17th at 7:00?"

"Yes, I can be there then."

"For music, does the P.A. System have a record player?"

"Yes, it does. Three speed."

"I thought we might have one musical piece before the processional and then something like a wedding march for the processional and no recessional. Just be with my friends."

"That sounds good. Now, here is a copy of my part of the service. I have made a little x here where I will give you time to say your own written part. Here is the address where you will need to go for your marriage license. Don't forget the documents. Can you think of anything else?"
"No," said Leit. Can you think of anything else, Gloria?"

"No, I think we have covered everything. Thank you so much, Rev. Burnett."

After supper that evening, Leit announced, "Now, I have a date with a beautiful woman! Do you happen to know to what I am referring, Mrs. Parsons?"

"I certainly do, Dr. Dorster! I believe the exact words were, 'It's a date, the very first night that we are back, after supper, this very spot!' And the spot referred to is the top of our hill!"

Leit and Gloria checked outside to be sure that it was completely dark and then walked, hand in hand, up the little path that went up the hill. The darkness was so dominant that Leit brought his torch to show the way. When they arrived at the top of the hill, Gloria sighed, "Leit, it is absolutely breath taking! It is almost as if you can reach out and touch the stars. Do you know what those few lights are in the distance?"

"Yes. The blinking green light to our starboard is from our little airport. The one single blinking red light is on the top of a telephone tower. The largest light, shaped like a cross, is on top of our school. Pilots have often told us that, on nights when they are looking for the airport – especially foggy nights – they often see the cross first and know that they are almost home. Rather symbolic, I think."

"That is beautiful, Leit. Now, do you remember when you had me close my eyes and you held my hand to show me my first glimpse of a Jamaican night sky?"

"How could I forget?" answered Leit. "It felt just as exciting as the first time I had the courage to hold a girl's hand!"

"I had the same emotional experience exactly, Leit. How uncanny! I remember that you had the courage, even at that early time, to share some of your feelings with me."

"I was really afraid that I had gone too far and too fast, Gloria. I was almost shaking with emotion."

"But I needed to hear those words, my Darling. I was having similar feelings and it frightened me that I might be out of line. Your words calmed my fears. I remember quoting Jim Stark that 'freedom and tyranny have within them the seeds of their own destiny'. I said that I believed that love also has within itself the seed of our knowing whether what we are experiencing is true love or not. And it proved to be so, Leit. When our plane crashed and I was sitting in that little rubber life raft, I knew beyond any doubt that my love for you was very real. All that I could think about was getting back to you."

"And the same was true for me, Gloria. When we were flying to London and wondering if you were safe, all I could think about was that I might have lost my chance to be with you for the rest of my life. Oh, it is so good to have you back! I never want to be that far away from you again!"

"Let's come up here often, Leit! Let's let this be our special place!"

"It will always be that, my Dear Gloria. Now, we might need to go back 'down to earth' for now, because we have a wedding to plan!"

"Yes. I can hardly wait! I am so happy, Leit! Thank you!" There was a kiss. This time it was not a "Clark Gable" kiss, but a quiet, very tender kiss that spoke volumes of what was in the hearts of two people who had been "surprised by joy".

The next morning Gloria said, "I guess we should call Thom and let him know that we have a date set for our wedding. "

"Right," said Leit. "Let's do it right now before we forget it." Leit dialed Thom and told him the good news.

"I will put that on my calendar and you can expect me. Someone on the crew will drive me over to Mandeville. I have good news for you also. Gloria's broker called from the real estate office yesterday and he said that he has sold your car and has the check for you. Would you want me to bring it?"

"Yes, definitely. That is good news. Tell him to call Gloria if he needs permission to give the check to you."
"Also, Leit, I saw on the government advisories that the English Ford that the flight crew has been using in Kingston is on the list of government sale items and the price is very reasonable. It only has 24000 kilometers (just under 15000 miles) registered, since it was used only about one day per week. So I will bring you the papers you would need to fill out in case you are interested."

"Oh, that sounds great, Thom. That sounds like a really good deal. We will probably do that! Thanks so much and we will look forward to seeing you."

"Isn't that great news, Gloria? Not only did they sell your Vauxhall, but we can get that gray English Ford for a good price. It really looked like new."

"Richard loved the English ford too! Isn't it wonderful, Leit, how everything is working out so nicely?"

On August 10, Leit got a call from Mrs. Keenan, of the Personnel Office at the Training School. "Dr. Dorster, this is Kathryn Keenan. Could you tell me how to get in touch with Mrs. Gloria Parsons? I know that she was planning to come back to Jamaica, but is she available now?"

"Only for a limited time, Kathryn. After August 19 she will only be available as Mrs. Leitman Dorster! "

"I heard about that, Leit. Congratulations. That is why I called. I want to talk with her about a position at the school!"

"Fabulous! I'll call her to the telephone."

"Hello, this is Gloria Parsons."

"Yes, this is Kathryn Keenan. On behalf of the Training School, I have been asked to offer you a teaching position. I presented your information to the Board of Directors and they have rescinded the usual requirement for a Bachelor level degree in favor of your two years of college if you agree to work, as your time permits, toward your Bachelor's degree. You would simply need it at whatever time it is required for us to meet the standards of a four year university. Could you agree with that?"

"Yes, I would have no problem with that."

"Then, what we have in mind for you is to begin this fall with one or possibly two courses. We would be starting our music curriculum based on your input and building on

it over several years. If you could definitely begin a course
in Music Appreciation this fall. We know that you play the
piano and have had some voice training. So, if you could
also have enough time to teach a second course of your
own choice this fall semester, that would be wonderful.
But, if you need more time you could begin that the next
semester or even next year. Then, as we have the funds to
do so, we will add another faculty member to the Music
faculty, with the goal of establishing a School of Music
within a few years. Now, the second subject that we had in
mind could be something like History of Music, or Basic
Music Theory – something like that."

"Mrs. Keenan, the prospects are very thrilling to anticipate.
I definitely would like to teach the Music Appreciation
Course. Let me see what texts are available, on short
notice, for a second class, and I will get back to you, say
by this time next week to allow me to call some book
companies. Thank you very much, Mrs. Keenan."

"Thank you for joining us, Mrs. Dorster to be!"

"Leit, can you believe it! I am going to be a teacher! With
you!"

Chapter 30. "The Wedding"

During the next several days, the trunk was delivered and
Gloria had it temporarily placed in the storage room, since
there was nothing in there that she would need
immediately.

One morning, while Gloria was gone to the store with
Cassia, Leit called Thom. He said again how glad he was
that Thom was coming and reminded him that they
expected him to spend that Thursday night with them.
Then he made a proposal to Thom, with the understanding
that, if it was too difficult, he should not give it another
thought. The proposal was: 1. If the Navy did not mind a
few more on the plane, and, 2. If Thom had time to call
Betsey, Clara, and Robert Swithers. 3. Invite all who
would be able to meet the plane with Thom, including
Charley, Elliott Swithers, and any of the Swithers family
that could get away. 4. The School would send a bus to the
airport in Kingston and meals and lodging would be
provided for all who could come and then they would be
taken back to the airport on Friday morning. He gave the
three telephone numbers to Thom and emphasized that if it
was going to take too much time and effort please don't do
it, but it would be a nice surprise for Gloria and Richard if
a few could come with him.

Thom, of course, took it as a major project, and the
response that he received from his several telephone calls
was an indication of how much the "message in the bottle"

had meant to all concerned. There were actually 11 who planned to come with Thom, including Betsey, Clara, Charley, and Bob Swithers' father, wife, son (Elliott), brothers, and a few cousins.

Leit asked Thom to call if and when he had a response and that, if Gloria were on the line for him to simply say that he was planning to come and that the plane crew would bring him to Mandeville if Leit could bring him back on Friday morning. But Leit also arranged for a secret code. Thom was to say, "The weather has been sort of messy here we have had x number of days of rain in a row. The x would indicate how many would be coming besides Thom. That would let Leit know how many to prepare for. If the x indicated no one else was coming Thom would say "the weather here has been unusually nice."

When Thom did call several days later, when Gloria was on the telephone, he told her the "good news" that he was going to be able to come to the wedding and that he would see her, Richard, and Leit by lunch time on Thursday. He said that he would have a ride to Mandeville. He said that he would welcome the nice weather in Jamaica, since it had been a bit messy in London, with rain every day for 11 days straight. Leit said, "Thank you for working it out to come, Thom. We will all be very glad to see you!" Gloria said, "I am so glad Thom is coming. It will be so nice to have someone come from London."

Leit smiled at the happy surprise that he was going to

spring on Gloria and Richard. Later he told Gloria that he needed to go over to the school to check about some things and while he was there he talked with the man in charge of the bus, who already knew of the plan, and gave him the number to expect. Leit then went by a local motel and arranged for rooms to accommodate 11 people. He would also take care of all meals. It would be somewhat expensive for Leit, but actually, no more expensive than most weddings. And he was more than happy to pay for anything that would make this a good experience for Gloria and Richard.

And so, by the Thursday before the wedding, all plans were in place for 12 friends of what might be called the "Message in the Bottle" project to show their love and appreciation to Richard and Gloria by traveling about 25 hours each way to attend a very important occasion in their lives.

Leit thought of another project also. One evening, after dinner, he said,"Gloria, I know that you and Richard gave up some of your wardrobe in order to come to Jamaica. You had to give up your heavy clothes simply because it does not get that cold here and you didn't feel that you had room to bring them in your suit cases. So, I would like for you both to think in terms of replenishing your clothes during the next several months. I would like for you to begin immediately with both of you getting new clothes for the wedding. Gloria, you get either a regular wedding dress or a really nice dress or suit and accessories. Richard,

I want you, likewise, to get a new outfit of your choosing. I will be glad to go with you both and I am sure that Cassia will lend a hand if you ladies prefer to go alone. Now, I do not mean to imply that I am going to tell you when to buy clothes and when not to – far from that. I am just trying to encourage you to do so."

"Thank you for being sweet and thoughtful, Dear. We will enjoy doing that."

Soon after they had talked with Rev. Burnett, Gloria and Leit were sitting in the living room and Gloria said, "How do you think we should go about writing our part of the ceremony, Leit?"

Leit suggested, "Why don't we each write out what we would like to say. Let's agree on, say 12 to 15 long hand lines and see if that is enough. When we have finished we can compare what was said, see if the styles harmonize and make any adjustments we need to make from there. What about that?"

"That should work," said Gloria. "Why don't we start tonight. We don't have anything pressing. That will give us more time to memorize than if we wait until later." Each of them took about 45 minutes. They compared and made a few style changes and felt that what they said would personalize and enhance the ceremony. Each part took about one minute. They decided to try to memorize their parts but would have a typed copy in their hand so if they were nervous they would have something to fall back on.

They decided that, for the music before the ceremony, they would play their favorite Rachmaninoff piece, "Rhapsody on a Theme of Paganini. They timed it and found that it would be much too long for folks standing for the ceremony and so they chose to play just the 18th variation, which was their favorite anyway. For the Processional it was a bit more difficult to decide. They listened to Mendelsohn's "Bridal March from A Midsummer Night's Dream", Bach's "Jesu, Joy of Man's Desiring", but settled on Wagner's "Bridal March" as being more appropriate for the setting of their hillside.

When the time came to go shopping for clothes, Gloria's practical side won out. She decided to buy a nice dress that she could wear to church on Sunday. Richard, likewise, chose to get a light weight sport coat, slacks, shirt, and, since the only shoes he brought were sandals and tennis shoes, he bought a nice pair of dress shoes.

The rehearsal was very informal and consisted primarily of a run through of how everyone was to walk, where they would stand, and especially, how the flower girl and ring bearer – Gabi and Consuela – would perform their duties without being afraid of making a mistake. Those girls were so proud of being "In Ms. Gloria's wedding". Gabi, especially, was so very glad that her "teacher" was going to be back for her class!

On the morning of the wedding, the bus left very early in the morning to meet the plane in Kingston. They had coffee, tea, and milk in large thermos jugs. They also had an assortment of doughnuts and sweet rolls. Clara had also, without telling anyone, smuggled a very large bag of her favorite goodies onto the plane and shared them on the bus. Everyone had plenty. Everyone on the bus was excited about their short but sweet vacation.

Gloria and Richard were told that they were meeting Thom at the Bloomfield Great House Restaurant. Leit had prepared Lou and Luigi for what to expect and they were going to "roll out the red carpet" for "Gloria's friends".

When the bus arrived at the restaurant they pulled around to the back so that Richard and Gloria would not see it.

Leit pulled up to the front entrance with Gloria, Richard, and Cassia. As they went in, Lou greeted them and said, "Well, how nice to see Gloria and Richard again, and on Thursday! As I recall it was on a Thursday that we first met you two. I will call Luigi. He will want to see you. "Oh, Luigi! Come, Gloria and Richard, follow me!" As they went through the door into the main dining room they heard,

"FOR SHE'S A JOLLY GOOD FELLOW, FOR HE'S A JOLLY GOOD FELLOW, FOR THEY ARE JOLLY GOOD FELLOWS....WHICH NOBODY CAN DENY!!!"

Gloria was absolutely beside herself. She yelled, she cried, she jumped up and down. Richard could not stop laughing. He thought it was the most perfect surprise that he had ever heard of. "How in the world did Dad and Thom pull this off!" he shouted.

When the excitement settled down, Lou showed Gloria and the others to their seats of honor. Everyone talked all during the wonderful luncheon. At the close, everyone was given a chance to say what was on their hearts and everyone at the table spoke. At the close, Gloria thanked everyone for honoring her and her family by coming this long distance to make their wedding complete. She finished by saying, "I thank God for looking down on three young men who were giving their all for their country, and using their last words as a seed to bring forth a garden of beautiful dreams in the lives of all of you and in the lives of me and my family. But it does not stop even with us, for it will continue to bloom in the lives of thousands, perhaps millions of young people who will be attending our School. And it will continue to bloom in your lives and in the lives of all who meet you – in your children, and in your children's children. I thank God and I thank you!"

Richard was last to speak. As he stood, his father, who was sitting next to him, pulled out the little bottle, which he had brought from Gloria's brief case. He passed it up to Richard, who had no idea at all that his father had it. He almost had to sit down because the impact of holding the bottle in the presence of all of these loved ones of those three men was so great....He held up the bottle to God and said, with a trembling voice, "Thank you, God, for trusting me with this..."

After the lunch, everyone was taken on a brief tour of some of the sights of the town and then by the school to see where Leit and Gloria would be teaching and where Richard would be a student. Then they were taken by their rooms to rest and get ready for the wedding. At 6:00 they were taken back to the school for a light sandwich supper that the faculty wives had prepared as their contribution to the wonderful surprise.

When the time came for the wedding, the people began gathering at 6:30. The bus parked in front of the Dorster home and everyone walked up to the top of the hill. Several men from the School had brought concrete blocks and two pieces of 4x8 plywood to make an 8ftx8ft. Platform. They draped this platform with a beautiful covering of off white material. It was just high enough so that those standing on the ground could see the ceremony easily.

The Minister stepped up on the platform at about 6:45 and checked the P.A. System. He then briefed a few of the people closest to the platform how to move back and form an aisle when the processional march began. At 6:50, The sounds of Rachmaninoff echoed softly over the crowd of about 200 people who were gathered around the platform. Gloria heard the strains from inside the house and was happy with their choice. At a certain point in the music the Minister made a "parting gesture" with his hands and an aisle began to open. The groom and the best man came and stood to one side just below the platform, just as the last strains of the Rachmaninoff were fading away.

The Processional began, the "Bridal Chorus from Wagner's Lohengrin", and all eyes were on a little girl who carried the rings on a beautiful satin pillow She beamed as she carried the pillow right up to the Best Man. These are often symbolic rings, but Leit and Gloria felt that Consuela might think that she was not trusted with the real rings and so the actual rings were tied with bows to the pillow. As she lifted the pillow, Richard carefully untied them and placed them in his hand. Then all eyes were on little Gabi, who smiled as she gracefully scattered flowers first to the right and then to the left, all the way up the hill. One girl stood to the right and one to the left. Then everyone beamed at the Maid of Honor, Cassia, as she walked gracefully up to Richard, who dropped the proper ring into her hand. Then she stood in her place on the other side.

At the point when the Bridal Chorus began again, All eyes looked at a beautiful Bride to be, on the arm of the man who had been, in recent days, most like a father to her, Sir Thomas Lawn, Commander, Royal Navy, ret. As the couple moved up to the wedding party, Sir Thomas stood between Gloria and Leit, as Cassia and Richard turned to face the Minister.

As they stood before the Minister, he held the microphone so that he could be heard, but if there was a response from anyone in the wedding party, he was careful to hold it to them so that everyone could be heard. He began:

"Dearly beloved, we are assembled here in the presence of God, to join this man and this woman in holy marriage; which is instituted of God, regulated by His commandments, blessed by our Lord Jesus Christ, and to be held in honor among all men." The Minister went on to charge the couple to be faithful and loving in their marriage. He then asked that God bless them today in the ceremony and then every day of their lives together.

Then, addressing Leit, he said, Leit, wilt thou have this woman to be thy wife, and wilt thou pledge thy self to her, etc.

Leit answered, "I will"

And Gloria, wilt thou have this man to be thy husband, and wilt thou pledge thy self to him, etc.

Gloria answered, "I Will"

Then the Minister said, "Who giveth this woman to be married to this man?

Thom said, "I do, a close family friend" Thom then steped back away from the wedding party and the wedding party stepped up before the Minister on the platform.

Then the Minister said, "Please hold hands and repeat after me the wedding vows.
"I Leit, take thee, Gloria, to be my wedded wife etc.

"I Gloria, take thee, Leit, to be my wedded husband etc.

Then the Minister said: "What words do you have to express the feelings that you bring to this Marriage

Leit: Dear Gloria: When you came into my life, I had thought that I was fairly happy. I had my teaching work, which I loved. I had my loving sister as my family. I thought that this was all that life would ever offer me. But, when I met you, I realized that this man, Leit Dorster, was on the threshold of a whole new life of love and challenge and opportunity that I thought belonged only to other men. I never dreamed that it could happen to me. But it has. You, Gloria, and my son, Richard, are the ones who have made this possible. I will love you both, and be the best husband and father that I can be for the rest of my life.

Gloria: Leit: In that same way that you describe, I had decided that is was enough to be a mother and a good realtor. I had my son and my work. I was fairly happy. But I saw other women who seemed to enjoy their relationship with their husband so much and I sometimes found myself wishing that I could have that added gift in my life. But I never expected that such a blessing would actually come to me, not until I met Leit Dorster. Then suddenly, as if it were a gift from God, I realized that I was being offered "almost Heaven" - at least as near Heaven as anything on earth can be. You, Leit, and I might add, you, Cassia, have let me see that God has chosen to give me more. I thank God, I thank Leit, I thank Richard, and I thank Cassia. Lastly I thank all of you – my new friends.

Then the Minister lead each in saying the vow of the rings and each received the rings from Richard and Cassia and placed them, without dropping a single ring, on the proper fingers.

Then there was a Prayer, asking that God bless the marriage of Leit and Gloria. It was true that everone present felt that God had already blessed them in many ways because of the multitude of things that had to "happen just exactly right" for them to have met and fallen in love as they had.

Then the Minister said to Leit, "You may kiss your bride." There was a momentary giggle that Gloria heard escape from Leit and she almost responded with another giggle. But she thought of the embarrassment that there would be if they went into that same giggle breakdown that had happened before, so she grabbed him and planted a kiss that would have made Clark Gable proud!

After the wedding they formed a reception line right there at the top of the hill and everyone had a good visit. Richard was glad to see the Rodriguez there and was able to have a few minutes with Jacqueline. The visitors from England were invited down to the house and given a quick tour and then everyone had refreshments and sat in the living room for another visit before the bus would take them back to the motel. Another group of volunteers, different from those who had taken the bus down the day before, prepared breakfast rolls, coffee, tea, and milk and picked up the visitors at 3:00 A..M. They had to leave that early in order to allow time for any delays on the road and then they would eat their breakfast when they were safely at the plane. Leit, Gloria, and Richard went with the visitors to Kingston. They had wonderful fellowship on the way. Thom gave them the check for the sale of their Vauxhall and also the papers to purchase the English Ford. In all of the activity he had almost forgotten that he had these in his pocket.

When the bus returned to the school, Gloria went in to see Kathryn Keenan and told her that she had found a good text for the second course. History of Music in Western Civilization.
As soon as they got back to their home, Gloria said, "Oh, Leit, let's walk back up on the hill!"

They almost ran up the hillside, hand in hand.

"As she gazed at the beauty all around her and smelled the breezes of Jamaica, Gloria said, "Leit. I think I am in Heaven! I believe I was born to be here. I think my whole life has been preparation for being with you – in Jamaica. I feel as though Jamaica is my real home! Thank you for bringing me back, Leit!"

"I would love to claim credit for that, Gloria, but in fact, it was God - and a little glass bottle."

Epilogue: "In fulfillment of my agreement with the Royal Navy, I wrote a full report on the experience that Richard and I had in carrying out our commitment to those three men who died in March of 1942. I sent the report to the Navy through Commander Thomas Lawn, our very good friend!

Gloria Parsons Dorster, Mandeville, Jamaica September, 1954"

THE END

Made in the USA
Charleston, SC
11 February 2013